CW01500219

ror shocked her at how fatigued she
mentioned anything to her? With the
Jackson, on the *Lexington*, it despera
that meant makeup! Georgia made a
for some tips.

The last two years living and working in the enclosed environment
of Alpha Base had clearly taken a toll on her. She couldn't recall noticing the rest of the crew looking as ragged as she now did. Perhaps she'd
not been paying them enough attention. That would need to change if
she wanted to create a good impression to Mars' new arrivals.

After shaking copious amounts of red dust from her hair, Georgia
made her way to the crew common room where the rest of the team
sat waiting for her. The room looked empty with only Joe Mancuso,
Megan Betts and Rashid Qadir. *Endeavour* had departed for Earth less
than a week ago and it was hard to reconcile that there were now only
four of the original twelve astronauts who had landed on Mars. Georgia put on her best fake smile and said, "Good morning, guys. Time for
the final inspection. Is there anything anyone wants to add before we
start?"

She looked around the room expectantly, but no one replied. Now
that she took time to notice, they were all as weary and untidy as she
was. All except Rashid, who still smiled and looked as enthusiastic and
smart as the day she had first met him on Earth at the start of mission
training. "Okay, in that case, let's move out."

First stop was the canteen area, next to the common room. Joe had
been responsible for this area so there were no surprises that the room
looked spotless, with all chairs neatly pushed under the tables. Ration
boxes stood neatly stacked on one side of the room and there was no
shortage of food. Most of it belonged to the deceased Captain Winter, Jim Grant, Tom Redmayne and Grace Cooke and remained largely untouched. For Georgia, it still seemed wrong to eat food prepared
for one of her fallen colleagues. But it could be a useful resource in the

event of a disaster. She hoped that they would never be in that situation, even though the odds weren't exactly favorable.

Joe stepped forward. "All appliances are fully operational. I have topped the freshwater tanks up, replaced filters, and tested for purity and mineral content. You can see the situation regarding ration packs," he said, nodding towards the far wall. "The only items we're running low on are coffee and powdered milk but there are about forty days' supply of each. I've cross checked all inventory on the computer systems and the only discrepancy was three packets of Orio's from Grace's rations."

"I confess. It was me," said Megan, sheepishly. "They were urgent medical supplies."

"No need to guess who the patient was," laughed Georgia. "I can't believe you didn't share them with me."

"It was an emergency," Megan insisted, with her sweetest smile.

"If you'll let me finish," Joe added. "We do have some fresh salad items from hydroponics, and I'll be gathering another crop in two days. So overall, we're in a good position. Especially when Expedition Three arrive with their supplies."

Georgia smiled encouragingly. "Thanks Joe, we want to make our new guests as welcome as possible. Good job."

The team made their way back through the common room and down one level via a spiral staircase. At the bottom, Georgia opened an airlock door that led to the original lava tube. She was still astonished at how much engineering had been involved to seal the opening and line the cave with aerogel before pressurizing it. Now, the crew could walk about without the need for environmental suits. Overhead lights and an array of heaters created a warm and welcoming environment. It made working so much easier and created an open space that didn't feel cramped or claustrophobic. The additional space had also dramatically improved the morale of everyone.

INCURSION

Book 2 of the Mars Frontier Series

Get the prequel to the Mars Frontier series FOR FREE

Sign up for the no-spam newsletter and get exclusive content, all for free.

Details can be found at the end of INCURSION.

COPYRIGHT

DEDICATION

To my family, for all their support on this journey

Chapter 1

The experience of riding her favorite chestnut pony, Conkers, through the woods just west of Denver was exhilarating to Georgia Pyke. She always liked to return here to get away from the stresses of modern life. The cold, crisp air took her breath away beneath a cloudless blue sky. Hidden birds sang and chirped, creating a soothing background music. The brown and russet leaves a sign that autumn was arriving early this year. Georgia couldn't remember being so relaxed as she gently swayed from side to side, safe in the knowledge that Conkers was familiar with this route. She'd been riding him since she was thirteen years old and he'd been the best birthday present her parents ever bought her.

She did, however, consider the distant glass spire standing taller than the mountains seemed out of place in the woods. Its glass windows reflected the mid-morning sun like an ancient lighthouse guarding the rocky shores. It looked oddly familiar, but she couldn't remember where she'd last seen it. As she stared more intently, she could see tiny craft buzzing around the spire, with some of them landing on the sheer sides. How was that possible? As she considered the problem, the sound of an approaching alarm interrupted her thought process. Why was there a siren in the mountains?

Blearily, Georgia realized that the morning alarm had wrenched her from the tranquility of her aunt's ranch in Colorado. She was still in her quarters in Alpha Base, laying on her bunk in the dark. The dream had been so vivid that she yearned to plunge back into it. Begrudgingly, she rolled out of bed, switched the light on in, looked at her reflection in the mirror and groaned. "You look like shit!" she scolded herself.

The dark bags under her eyes, together with the increasingly unwelcome number of crow's feet, made her look ten years older. An explosion of spots covered her deathly pale skin. Her hair was wild, unkempt and desperately in need of some styling. It was the first time in months she'd taken a good look at herself and the reflection in the mir-

After twenty yards, the lava tube opened up into a large cavern containing the science labs, aquaponics and living quarters. The next stop on the tour was the new living quarters. They had been created using the 3D printers and Martian regolith to create a structure that was two stories tall and could house fifty people comfortably in individual cabins. Capacity could be expanded in the future, but that was unlikely to be for another two years. Showers and toilets were yet to be installed with the existing facilities still located in the old inflatable modules.

Again, Georgia was fascinated with what she saw. Although she had visited the living quarters during their construction, she had yet to move in and she had not seen the individual rooms in their completed state. As base commander, her quarters were currently in the new part of Alpha Base, below the control room, and she appreciated she'd have to make way for her incoming replacement. She made a mental note to put her name on one of the new rooms. She deserved first pick, after all.

Before leaving the living quarters, she asked Rashid, "What is the situation with the 3D printers? Have you discovered the problem?"

"It's the usual situation. Buildup of foreign objects in the mechanism has caused some erosion. I've cleaned as much as I can, but the damage is too severe. I'll replace them with the spare parts being delivered by *Lexington*. The construction robots have gathered enough raw material so we can restart building operations within the next week to ten days." Rashid gave the report in his usual annoying upbeat manner. *I want whatever he's eating*, thought Georgia.

Mancuso added. "It's the same story for all equipment exposed to the Martian dust. You've seen the evidence Georgia. Hopefully, the guys back at Houston can design better and more resilient equipment for future missions."

Georgia nodded. "General Stockton is fully aware of the situation and has the best engineers on the case. But you're still looking at two years away. For now, we must make the new batch of spares last as best we can although there will be less construction required in the near future."

"Do you know what spares Captain Bailey is bringing with him?" asked Rashid.

"I don't have the full list. For some reason, the general hasn't shared that information. I have been assured that all the equipment and spares we asked for ten months ago is being provided. But as the attrition rate on equipment has increased since then, we're still going to be struggling to keep everything working when Expedition Four arrives."

"I'll be less conservative next time I complete a requisition," replied Rashid.

"I doubt we'd have been allowed much more. My understanding is they loaded the supply ships with mining equipment. The mining companies who invested in the Mars program are looking for returns on their investment."

"That's good news for us," said Megan thoughtfully. "If the companies find the minerals they're looking for, then it gives us a chance of being successful long term. We'll have something to trade and Earth will continue sending supplies."

"I know. I have bigger plans for this planet to become more than just one large mining operation though. It has to be a steppingstone for the rest of the solar system, and then the Universe. The lower gravity makes Mars an ideal location as a spaceport. Better still, we could use one of the moons."

Megan sighed. She'd heard this fanciful dreaming enough times. "Georgia, I know you're impatient and not willing to wait for the alien civilizations to come to us. But you have to be realistic. We've been here two years and not even scratched the surface of what may be possible on this planet. You need funding and a huge amount of long-term commitment from industry and government. And who are you to say that expanding across the cosmos is going to be a positive experience?"

"I know you think I'm fixated. Maybe I am. But is it wrong to have ambitions for the whole of humanity, not just for myself?"

"It is a very honorable goal," replied Rashid. "I want to know and understand what advanced technology exists out there. I would also like to experience new cultures and understand if religion is a universal belief."

"Great!" said Megan, sardonically. "Georgia, you've made a disciple out of our chief engineer. You're one person, out of seven billion who exist on a small remote planet. How are you ever going to achieve your goals?"

"By continuing to believe. If it's meant to be, it will happen. I don't know how but an opportunity will present itself. For now, can we get back to business? We have guests arriving." And with that she led the crew to complete the base inspection.

Chapter 2

Georgia stared through the large panoramic window at the desolate Martian plain beyond. From her vantage in the newly completed control room she could see for miles. To her right were the two remaining supply ships and the solar farm. Straight ahead, about five miles away stood the remains of *Eden,* which had been cannibalized for spare parts, including this huge window. All that was left beneath the metallic latticework were the massive rocket engines and two oxidizer tanks.

In the far distance, Georgia spotted several dust devils dancing across the landscape. They always seemed to appear at this time of day, brought to life temporarily by the sun heating the ground. With their ephemeral nature and complex erratic movements across the plains, she thought they should be called faeries instead of devils. She had a soft spot for them and, on some days, even gave them individual names.

Mancuso was relaxing in Georgia's command chair, reading the latest news from Earth on the computer screen in front of him. He looked up at Georgia's silhouette against the window. "You've been standing there for at least ten minutes," he said. "Don't you ever get tired of the view? All I've seen for two years is red dust and brown rocks. I miss blue skies and green grass. Even the occasional rain shower would be a welcome change."

"That's where we differ, Joe," she replied. "I see the future. And I wonder that we've achieved so much in such a short time. Can you imagine how this will be transformed in the next five to ten years? This could be a thriving city by then, with hundreds of humans living here. Maybe even families. The start of a Martian civilization."

"Perhaps I'm not a dreamer like you but I don't doubt this place will change. I know you don't like the idea, but I'm convinced it will be nothing more than a mining colony. We've all seen the plans. And the place will look even more desolate with quarries and heavy mining equipment. It will be a place to work, not to live."

Georgia moved to the control console and sat on a chair facing Mancuso. "I hope you're wrong about that. I know there will be a vast mining enterprise because we need the funding. But don't you think there has to be more we can do here? Wouldn't you like to create something special you can be proud of? To demonstrate what can be achieved beyond financial balance sheets and returns on investment."

Mancuso laughed out loud. "Now I know you're dreaming. I doubt the Russians and Chinese have your sensibilities. They're coming here to dig for minerals too, to make a profit for their investors. Nothing more. And there's no one to oversee who owns which bit of real estate. Do you think we can even all live in harmony? We don't speak to the Russian and Chinese scientists on the other side of the planet as it is."

Georgia sighed. She knew there was a lot of truth in what Mancuso had just said. She had tried on a number of occasions to arrange meetings with the other science base, but they had refused to co-operate. It reflected the geopolitical landscape on Earth, and she was desperate to change it. She wasn't sure that *Lexington*'s captain held her views either.

"Maybe you're right Joe. After our experiences with the Sentinels, I really believed the knowledge we weren't alone in the Universe would change how politicians perceived each other. That it would create some kind of harmony amongst nations that would be positive for mankind. I've seen none of that."

"That's because those same politicians fear losing their power and influence. The status quo suits them. Especially when the reality is that we won't encounter an alien civilization for hundreds if not thousands of years. Politicians are short sighted and only concerned with the next election. Why do you think they've never shared the news with the public?"

"Then where is the hope for our future? Something has to change. Surely you can see that? We can't have finished developing as a species. We've sacrificed so much just to get a toehold on this planet. I don't want the lives we've lost to have been in vain."

Mancuso was about to respond when the communications equipment lit up. He leaned over and pressed a button on the screen in front of him. "Alpha Base, this is *Endeavour*," came the voice of Emily Pope through the speaker.

Georgia and Mancuso looked at each other and smiled. Emily, as always, was punctual with everything she did. "Hi Emily," replied Mancuso. "Are you calling to ask for directions?"

There was a short delay before the response came through. "You'd be the last person I'd ask if I was lost. We're still on the correct trajectory and all systems remain nominal. Nothing much to report since my previous transmission."

Endeavour had departed for Earth six days earlier, along with two supply ships, Intrepid and Challenger, that were loaded with enough samples and completed experiments to keep Earth scientists occupied for decades. On board were pilot Emily Pope and biologists Harry and Nicola King. So far, the journey had been uneventful, and they were looking forward to gently coasting back home in a little over two months. Although he'd never admit it, Mancuso was missing the friendly banter he had with Pope. But she had always planned to return to Earth and there was no one else to pilot the ship.

"Harry and Nicola are both worried that you've killed their plants already. They've asked me to remind you to clean the filters and to test the mineral levels in the hydroponics tanks. I'm sure you know what you're doing but would appreciate confirmation and maybe some photographic evidence."

"Hi Emily, it's Georgia. You can assure the Kings that I carried out an inspection of the base earlier today and the hydroponics are looking as they did one week ago. Mancuso is following Harry's detailed instructions to the letter. And I, for one, am grateful that we still have fresh produce."

"They'll be pleased to hear that. They've been in their rooms writing several research papers and fretting at having left their work to amateurs."

"Amateurs!" spluttered Mancuso. "I spent three long months with them, being shown how to use the equipment, understanding which plants required certain minerals and how to test for saline levels. They watched my every move once I was inside their aquaponics world. I lost count of how many books they made me read. Just so I could be called an amateur. It's outrageous."

After several seconds pause, all Mancuso and Georgia could hear over the radio was hysterical laughter. "I'm sorry Joe, I couldn't help myself. They never called you amateur. In fact, the Kings have sung your praises, which is really quite annoying. They think, with the dedication you've shown, you could have a future as a horticulturist."

Mancuso saw the funny side. After all, he'd caught Emily out several times so he should have expected she'd have her revenge at some point. "Good one, Emily. I think that now makes us even."

"Not by a long way. You must have a short memory if you've forgotten the pranks you've played on me. Luckily, I have a very good memory, and just over two months to think about what I can tell the press about our time together. I'm sure I can have some fun with them at your expense."

Mancuso was temporarily horrified. He looked up at Georgia, who was stifling a grin. "She wouldn't do that would she? She's not allowed. My family would see it on TV and believe anything she said."

Georgia shrugged. "Keep me out of it. If you didn't think she'd pay you back for the ribbing you gave her, then you don't understand women. You may think we don't hold grudges, but we do."

"But it was all in good fun," he protested. He pressed the comms button again, attempting to sound laid back. "Nicely played Emily. We had some fun while you were here, but I think we both know it stopped when you took off six days ago. I hope we get another opportunity to catch up for some friendly banter when I return to Earth in only two years."

Emily was still laughing at his expense. "If I'd know you were so easy to wind up, I'd have done more when I was on Mars. That's going to be one of my biggest regrets. Other than having to leave you guys. Maybe I should return. Anyway, I'll sign off for now. I'm sure you're busy rolling out the red carpet for *Lexington*'s crew. Say hi to them from me. Pope out."

Georgia looked suspiciously at Mancuso. "Are you sure you and Emily never hooked up? There was an awful lot of underlying sexual tension in that conversation."

"Don't be ridiculous," Mancuso protested, almost too much. "We're just good mates. Emily wouldn't have been interested in me in that way. Would she?"

Georgia smiled and headed toward the door. "I guess you'll never know."

Chapter 3

Lexington and its convoy of four supply ships were now less than one day from Mars. Captain Mackenzie 'Mac' Bailey was in his quarters, reviewing the latest reports from his senior staff. So far, the mission had been largely uneventful, bordering on dull. But with all craft scheduled for a landing at Alpha Base at around nine o'clock the following morning, anticipation was building.

Captain Bailey was a NASA veteran and had been an astronaut for over twenty years. He had been the CAPCOM for the fateful Expedition One eight years earlier. When that mission had failed in such a catastrophic and tragic manner, he feared that he would never get the opportunity to travel to Mars. In the end, he was one of the lucky ones to escape any censure in the subsequent inquiry that identified the failings that led to the deaths of the four astronauts. For a long time after the inquiry, however, there was considerable doubt whether the Mars program should continue at all. There had been a great deal of public debate around the cost and safety of sending people to Mars and bringing them home again.

When NASA had unexpectedly selected him to command Expedition Three, he had spent many weeks deliberating whether he should accept the appointment. It had been something he'd desired for a long time prior to the loss of Expedition One. He discussed the options with his wife and children before finally agreeing to lead the mission. He'd been involved closely in the consultation process for the safety changes implemented by NASA and the government and had seen at first hand that no stone was left unturned to ensure the spaceship upgrades were implemented correctly. The success of Expedition Two had provided him with the final reassurance he needed. Since then, the development program for the Mars missions had continued apace. Even though it was only two years newer, *Lexington* was a far superior ship to the *Endeavour* or *Eden*, with additional radiation shielding, better flight computers and an updated life support system which had allowed for twenty astronauts to be accommodated this time around.

Despite the strain of the previous eight years, Mac had never lost his sense of humor. These days, though, he was more cautious who he opened up to. Being captain meant that he had to show decorum and seniority at all times. His engaging personality and charisma, however, had made him popular with the public and NASA's public relations team.

As Mac finished the reports, Lieutenant Charlie Molloy knocked on the captain's door and asked, "are you ready for us now, sir?" Behind Molloy, Paige Duncan popped her head up and smiled at Captain Bailey.

Bailey glanced at the clock on the wall. "Sorry Charlie, yes come in. You too, Paige," he said, mildly embarrassed. "I hadn't realized the time."

Charlie Molloy was a small man, about five inches shorter than Bailey and proudly boasted to anyone who would listen that he would be the first ginger person on Mars. He'd said it so many times it had become a running joke. He was one of the mission specialists and had been seconded from the army because of his particular expertise.

Paige Duncan, on the other hand, was far more reserved and quieter. As Chief Scientist for the mission, she was dedicated to achieving a number of experiments set by her colleagues back on Earth. She saw this mission as a huge opportunity to further her career, even if it meant tolerating loud mouths such as Charlie. If it wasn't for the fact he was such an expert in his field, she would have nothing to do with him. It was no secret amongst the crew, however, that she had a fondness for the captain. She continually flirted with him yet Bailey, a strong family man, chose to either ignore her advances or they passed him by entirely.

Bailey looked across at the pair of them. "Paige, do you mind closing the door? I know it's a squeeze in here, but I don't want this conversation shared with any other member of the crew."

"Of course, sir," she replied, conspiratorially. "I understand."

Molloy smiled to himself but said nothing. He wondered how the captain couldn't notice her blatant flirting.

Once the door was closed, Bailey continued. "Thank you both for making some time. I know you're both busy preparing for the landing so I will keep this meeting short. This morning, I received updated orders from General Stockton. The administration is concerned that both the *Moskva* and the *CSS Shandong* have closed in range over the last week and are now less than twenty-four hours behind us. There's little doubt that the Russians and the Chinese want to be the first to test the weapons we know they are carrying. Of course, that is still conjecture with neither country confirming nor denying their intentions may be other than peaceful exploration."

"That's bullshit and everyone knows it," interrupted Molloy. "Everyone knows they're here to test out their new weaponry. That's one of the reasons we're here too."

Bailey held his hand up. "Calm down, Charlie. Yes, we all know it's a game of smoke and mirrors. No nation is publicly going to declare their true intentions are they. Can you imagine the public outcry? The public thinks their tax dollars are being spent on positive initiatives."

Paige said, "none of this is new, Mac. What does Stockton expect us to do?"

"They want us to start our testing program at the earliest opportunity. Certainly within the next week. We have to be first to test our particle beam. Is that possible?"

Molloy and Paige looked hesitantly at each other, waiting for the other person to speak. It was Paige who offered her opinion. Frowning, she said, "Yes it's achievable, Mac. Once the equipment is unloaded, it should take no more than two days to set up plus maybe another day to calibrate and shake out any minor issues. That's on the basis that nothing is damaged during landing."

"The issue is retaining secrecy," added Molloy. "We'll need to keep everyone else away from *Yorktown* for as long as possible."

"We've programmed the landing sequence so that *Yorktown* is furthest from Alpha Base. No one should need to go there without a good reason," confirmed Bailey. "This has always been a need to know exercise."

"Once we start testing, it's going to be difficult to keep it secret for long," said Paige. "We're going to have to draw power from Alpha's reactor to charge the batteries. That means running several miles of cable and plugging it into the existing transmission lines. Pyke or their chief engineer, Qadir, is soon going to spot that. We may even require their assistance."

"It won't matter by then. Once the weapon test has begun, then nothing can stop it. And we'll have grabbed a march on the others," replied Bailey.

"Agreed sir," said Molloy. "If you can keep Pyke occupied for the first few days then I'm sure Paige and I can get the weapon assembled and ready for the first test firing. By then it's going to be far too late for anyone to object. If the information leaks, then it will demonstrate to the Russians and Chinese that we won't be walked over on Mars any more than we have been on Earth. We'll be able to defend ourselves from any threats."

Bailey was less confident. "Remember, this is an experimental weapon only. If successful, we can then scale up for a planetary defense capability. There is no intention to make it an offensive weapon."

Molloy held Bailey's stare. "Of course not, sir. But we are planning for every eventuality. Surely we've learned to be ready for the unexpected. Who knows if the next challenge will come from Earth or space?"

"I sometimes think you know more than you're sharing with me, Charlie." Bailey had had suspicions for a while that he wasn't completely in the loop. Although Molloy reported directly to him, there had been the odd occasion when Molloy seemed to be receiving direction from elsewhere. Maybe it was simply Molloy's arrogance. Bailey had learned to trust his instincts and there was something he couldn't get to the bottom of.

Molloy shrugged innocently. "I doubt that very much, sir. We're reporting everything we do directly to you."

Paige look confused by the discussion. "So, we're all agreed that we can get the particle beam ready within the next seven days. We will need some help to unload the test equipment. It is bulky and I don't think the two of us can handle it, especially during the time we acclimatize to Martian gravity."

"I'd forgotten about that," conceded Bailey. "Okay, leave that with me. I may need to get Mancuso's help. He was loadmaster for the previous Expedition. "I'll send my recommendations to Stockton. In the meantime, you're dismissed."

Once he was alone again, Bailey stared at the now open door. The weapons test troubled him. Not just the secrecy surrounding it but the fact that this was a quasi-military operation. The more he thought about it, the more uneasy he felt that the military was interfering with space exploration and that wasn't something he'd signed up for. If it wasn't for the fact that the Russians and Chinese were following a similar path, he would have put up a stronger argument against the tests. All he could do now was keep a close eye on the testing schedule.

***

Jackson Pyke was on *Lexington*'s flight deck staring out at Mars. Every day was bringing him closer to his sister. He hadn't seen Georgia since saying goodbye to her twenty-eight months earlier, three days before she had departed for Mars. Since then, he had avidly followed her progress and been in awe when he first saw the images of her be one of the first set foot on a new planet. Although they had regularly spoken via video messages, it wasn't the same thing. He could feel the emotions building inside of him and hoped that he could hold it all together when he got to see her. She meant more to him than Mars ever could.

"Hey Jackson, can you see your sister yet?" joked Paige as she floated up behind him to take in the view.

"You're hilarious, Paige. I was admiring the planet and imagining
what it would be like finally to escape this rocket. Don't you find it
claustrophobic after three months?"

She nodded, "there are some people I would like to get a break
from. With twenty people you're going to find some are more annoying
than others." She winked at him to let him know she wasn't being serious.

Even though Paige was ten years older, Jackson had a crush on her.
He wasn't sure if it was her bright blue eyes, radiant smile or confident
aloofness. There was just something about her that attracted him to her.
Twice during training, he had invited her out for drinks and each time
she had refused. He felt a pang of jealousy each time he saw the way
she spoke to Captain Bailey. Yet he couldn't help the way he felt. All he
could do was try to hide it from her.

"Have you packed up your science labs ready for tomorrow?" he
asked, knowing full well that she had but keen to keep her on the flight
deck as long as possible.

"Yes, that was finished first thing this morning. I've triple checked
that everything is secure as I don't know how rough the landing will be.
To be honest, entry and landing are the only parts that truly scare me.
It's what has kept me awake for the past few nights."

"I know what you mean," Jackson lied. The thrill seeker in him
couldn't wait to hurtle through the Martian atmosphere before the
rockets slowed them for landing. But he could still be sympathetic. "It
is the most dangerous part of the mission, but the ship seems to have
held up well so far and there have been more successful landings than
failures."

Paige grimaced. "I'm not sure you're helping, Jackson. I assume
you're totally prepared for arriving on Mars. All of your equipment is
on *Argonaut*."

"Yes, I'm keen to get some work done, finally. There's only so much remote research that I can do. It will be great to get out on the planet rather than analyze satellite imagery and thermal imagery. I may even need your assistance with testing soil specimens."

"Good luck with that. My time for the next two years is already fully accounted for. I may let you use some of my equipment if you ask nicely but otherwise, you're on your own. I'm sure your sponsors have ensured you are fully equipped anyway. They'll want to see a quick return on their investment."

"That's true. They're hoping I find the elements that create the next gold rush. Mars offers huge potential for minerals that are becoming scarce and therefore expensive. I'm focused on finding deposits of gold, platinum and titanium but if I can discover any viable deposits of rare elements, then I will be equally rewarded."

"And I guess you're also keen to meet up with your sister again. You must have missed her."

"I am so proud of what she has achieved so far. I never expected she would be commanding the outpost for two years. She's never sought glory or leadership, but she's stepped up to the mark when her country needed her. She's always just been my big sister"

"Haha. I can imagine you were a handful."

"I've had my moments," he conceded. "I'm different now. I know what I want and how to focus on what's important to me." He looked towards Paige, but she was now distracted by the view and didn't notice.

Just my luck, he said to himself. Although he understood deep down that Paige only had eyes for the captain, he would not give up. That wasn't his style. He watched her for another couple of moments, noticing how the edges of her mouth curled up in a smile and her eyes sparkled in the sunlight, before dragging himself away, back to his cabin to get some rest prior to the landing.

Chapter 4

"Well, this is our last night of peace, Meg. It all changes as of tomorrow when *Lexington* arrives." Georgia sat back in her chair and took a long sip of hot chocolate from her favorite mug. It was now just the two of them sitting in the common room after dinner. Mancuso and Rashid had disappeared for the evening, probably to their quarters to message family.

Megan sat with a glass of orange juice. "I know you're not keen on change, Georgia. I don't think I am. But we have to accept that the base needs to expand. We're all tired. We've struggled for two years with being seriously under manned. As chief physician, I've seen the emotional and physical impact on everyone, including you. If we were on Earth, we'd all be hospitalized. On top of that, most of our external equipment has been damaged or destroyed by the harsh Martian climate and needs replacing or repairing. We can't go on much longer and the *Lexington* cannot arrive soon enough."

Georgia sighed. "I know all that. And without the supplies being delivered tomorrow, we'd be on *Endeavour* heading back to Earth too. Our survival is so precarious at the moment. It's unsettling. Yet we've made this our home. I feel territorial and don't want to share it with newcomers who may not have the same motivations as we do. I'm sure I'll be okay after a few days and I get to know Captain Bailey and his crew."

"It could have been far worse," Megan said dryly. "If the Hornet hadn't developed issues shortly before it was set to leave Earth orbit then we would be expecting forty people. How would you have coped then?"

"Good point. I'll let you know in another two years when the next colonists arrive."

"You intend to stay for good then?"

22

"Yes, I thought you would have guessed that by now. I have bigger visions for Mars, although I need to clear them with General Stockton. I was hoping maybe you would consider staying permanently."

Megan shook her head. "No. I agreed to stay on an extra deployment to help you out, but my place is back on Earth. I'll be on board the next transit ship in two years. Four years will be more than enough time for me."

"We'll see," laughed Georgia. "I'll make a Martian out of you yet."

"I thought you'd be excited for the *Lexington* to arrive. Surely you want to see Jackson again."

"Yes, it's hard not to think about anything else. We have a lot of catching up to do. There's so much he doesn't know about my time here. I either couldn't find the right time to share the news and security concerns prevented me from sharing too much information."

"Wow! You do have a lot to talk about. And no doubt he has his own adventures to share with you."

"Quite possibly. But probably not as big as mine. I've felt guilty and a coward at not sharing what's happened to me. But how do I tell him that an advanced extraterrestrial civilization saved me? It all sounds so far-fetched."

"How do you think Jackson will take the news?"

"I've played the conversation in my head so many times, trying to figure the best approach. I know he'll accept whatever I say with sympathy. I don't know how he'll take the fact that we're not alone in the Universe. It's something we didn't discuss. I'd never given alien life any serious consideration until I bumped into them."

"Do you still think about the Sentinels?" asked Megan.

"Every day! They changed me forever. Not only did they save my life, but they gave me the briefest glimpse behind the curtain. The possibilities are endless, and the knowledge is driving me mad. I sometimes wish I'd not met the Sentinels, or think they should have left me to die. Not knowing the truth of their existence would be so much easier. Instead, I have a burning need to find them again. And the only way to do that is to prove that mankind is ready to be part of the Confederacy."

Megan could see the anguish in Georgia's eyes as she spoke. "I understand some of what you feel. I know I could save more lives if only I had access to the advanced medical equipment that must be available. It's frustrating but if I turned that emotion into an obsession, I wouldn't be able to do my job properly. You need to be realistic and careful that you're not consumed by your desire. I don't want you to grow old and die disappointed. So much of humanity's destiny is entirely outside your control."

"I'm not obsessed, Megan. Dedicated would be a better description. It's the memories that drive me. The events that took place feel like they happened only yesterday. Sending Jim away with the Sentinels is still raw. At the time I was sure it was the right thing to do, but I relive those moments every night before I go to sleep. When I look up at the stars, I wonder if Jim is out there and if he blames me for sending him to some distant point out there."

"We've been over this countless times. You saved Jim's life, Georgia. How could he resent you for that? If you hadn't allowed the Sentinels to take him, then he would have died. There was absolutely nothing I could do for him. His injuries were far too severe. None of it was your fault."

"A sign would be nice. To show that he survived or that we're on the right path as a species."

"You can't go on wondering whether the choices you made were the correct ones. We have twenty new people arriving tomorrow, all with their own ambitions and dreams. Your time is better spent focusing on them."

"I don't know any of them. Will any of the new arrivals align with my ideals and make this planet a better place?"

"Georgia, everyone on board *Lexington* wants to turn Mars into a habitable human colony. Otherwise they wouldn't be coming. Some will even intend to settle here, like you. Give them the benefit of the doubt and allow them time to adjust. You must let them decide their own opinions of Mars before you can tell them your own thoughts and intentions. Isn't the concept of trust a key pillar of your plans?"

She shrugged in submission. "You're right, Megan. It is. How can I expect people to trust in me when I don't demonstrate that trait? You're a wise doctor and the best friend I could hope for. My nerves have made me impatient. Thank you for showing me my flaws."

"It's not a flaw, Georgia. You're overworked and exhausted. As your doctor, I prescribe some rest. We have a busy day tomorrow."

Georgia didn't argue. She was feeling very weary and overwhelmed. She wished Megan a good night before ambling back to her quarters for a sound sleep.

Chapter 5

Georgia and the remaining members of Expedition Two convened in the control room at ten o'clock the following morning. There was a buzz of excitement that they had not felt for a long time, together with a subtle sense of anxiety that the status quo was shifting. It reminded Georgia of the first day of training when she was waiting to meet who would join her on Expedition Two. Any negativity she'd been feeling was pushed to one side for the day. It was time to celebrate the arrival of new friends. And, of course, her brother.

Earlier that morning, the four of them had started the day together in the gym. It had been a relaxed work out with plenty of banter as the crew unconsciously bonded together to prepare for the day ahead. Each of them temporarily forgot the stresses and strains of the previous two arduous years as they shared their positive experiences of life on Mars. Long hot showers followed exercise before finding the cleanest clothes to wear. None of them had been this tidy in months, even the impeccable Rashid Qadir.

Joe Mancuso had spent the past ten minutes in communication with *Lexington*'s pilot. "Entry burns went like clockwork. *Lexington* entered the upper atmosphere eleven minutes ago and is tracking perfectly, with the supply ships following in an orderly procession. Flight surfaces are starting to experience drag, but no more than expected. This should be some show Captain Bailey puts on for us."

Georgia looked out of the large viewing window and knew that he was right. The sun had risen above the horizon three hours earlier and was high in the sky, enabling a perfect view of the ships as they arrived. She picked up a pair of binoculars that were resting on the console next to her and focused in on the landing platform they had built for *Lexington*, only a short distance from where *Endeavour* had stood about three miles from Alpha Base. The ground had been leveled and smoothed over to ensure *Lexington* had an ideal place to land with no debris that might fly up and damage one of the rocket engines.

Tracking the binoculars up and to her left, Georgia noticed that the sky was remarkably clear. There were no signs of any dust storms that plagued Mars on a regular basis. *This should make it easier to spot Lexington*, she thought.

Within twenty seconds she saw the first signs of *Lexington* as it came into view. At first all she could see was a vapor trail but then she caught the odd flash as the sun reflected off the gleaming metal of the spacecraft. Several seconds later, Georgia could see that *Lexington* was performing standard maneuvers to slow its speed, ready for landing. The ship was like a silver bullet, racing across the orange sky. She remembered her own feelings during her own landing on *Endeavour* and wondered if everyone on board was as nervous as she had been.

For a moment it appeared as if *Lexington*'s pilot would overshoot the landing pad. At the last minute, however, the ship's nose pitched up to slow its horizontal speed and *Lexington* executed a flawless landing, throwing up a large plume of dust and exhaust smoke as it majestically settled onto the Martian surface. Despite the distance to *Lexington*, Georgia could feel the vibrations through her feet and the large viewing window shook in its mounts.

"I'm not sure I could ever tire of watching that," said Mancuso. "How amazing is it that mankind can launch a rocket, send it millions of miles across the solar system and land it with pinpoint accuracy and within three seconds of its scheduled time. My train to work was never that punctual, and it was only a thirty-minute journey."

The comms channel suddenly burst to life with Captain Bailey's exuberant voice. "Good morning Alpha Base. I hope we put on a good show for you all. It's not every day you have spaceships landing on your doorstep"

"Hi Mac, it was spectacular," replied Georgia. "Welcome to Mars. You made that look very easy. I can't tell you how glad we all are to have you here with us."

"The feeling's mutual. We'll commence our post flight checks and will be ready for collection around midday."

"Roger that. In the meantime, we'll sit back and enjoy the rest of the show. I would highly recommend that you take some time out to watch the arrival of your supply ships."

Georgia flicked the radio off and returned to the viewing window just in time to see the first of the supply ships come into land less than five miles away to the east. She stayed by the window and watched as the remaining three supply ships landed at regular five-minute intervals, all without a hitch. Unfortunately, the final two landings were hidden by the large cloud of dust created by the earlier landings.

"That was too easy," said Megan. "It's a testament to the reliable and safe system we've developed. I'll have fewer fears when I return to Earth."

Megan's remark didn't go unnoticed by Georgia. She was more than up for the challenge to convince Megan to stay.

***

Because only one of the two Mobile Extravehicular Vehicles, or MEVs, was operational, they hitched a trailer to it to ferry some of *Lexington*'s astronauts back to Alpha Base. Even then, three trips were going to be required, with Mancuso acting as the driver. Georgia felt it appropriate she should also go out to greet Captain Bailey and welcome him formally.

As the MEV pulled up at one of *Lexington*'s landing legs, Georgia spotted the first group of six astronauts descending from the cargo bay in the cradle. They were each wearing bright clean white mobility suits that wouldn't stay that color once they'd spent a few weeks on Mars.

"Watch this," she said to Mancuso as Captain Bailey prepared to take his first tentative steps on the Martian surface. He was holding on tightly to the cradle's safety bar, obviously still getting accustomed to Martian gravity.

Mancuso laughed. "That takes me back. It reminds me of watching my own children learning to walk when they were about one-year-old."

They both continued to watch patiently through the MEV's front window as Captain Bailey cautiously led his crew towards them, their faltering steps no more than a shuffle as they traveled the ten yards from the cradle to the MEV's airlock.

Georgia leaned forward in her seat to try to identify Jackson. With their visors down to protect against the sun's rays, it was impossible for her to identify which of the astronauts could be Jackson. As they shambled slowly past the MEV's window though, it didn't take long to know that none of them was Jackson. Disappointed, she sat quietly brooding and hoping that it wouldn't be too long before he emerged.

***

Five minutes later, Bailey and three of his colleagues exited the airlock into the rear of the MEV. Bailey removed his helmet, ran his fingers through his thinning gray hair and smiled at Georgia and Mancuso. "Georgia Pyke, I presume," he said. "I've come a long way to see you."

Georgia shook his hand warmly and was surprised at how firm his grip was. "Hello Captain Bailey. Gravity's a bitch ain't it? I'd forgotten its effect until a few minutes ago. You'll be fine in a few days but it's gonna hurt. Luckily it's nowhere near as bad as returning to Earth after several weeks on the Moon."

Bailey slumped into his seat as if to confirm Georgia's statement. "This is the part I've been dreading most," he replied. "The three-month transit time and precision landing was a piece of cake compared to trying to walk again."

"We'll get you back to Alpha as quickly as possible. Joe here has volunteered to act as chauffeur for the day and will shuttle the rest of your crew from *Lexington*."

"Much appreciated. If you're wondering about your brother, he'll be part of the next group. He's desperate to see you but wanted to collect several personal items, rather than leave them on the ship."

"That sounds like Jackson," replied Georgia. "He's always been the organized one. To be honest, it'll will be easier to say our hello's in the privacy back at base rather than the confines of this vehicle in front of you all."

As Mancuso started the MEV for the return journey to the base, Captain Bailey nodded in understanding. "Let me introduce you to some of my crew." Three people were sitting in the remaining seats at the rear of the cabin with a strange mixture of fatigue and exhilaration on their faces. "This is Professor Paige Duncan. She's chief scientist and will take over the vacant role that you've lacked for some time."

Georgia felt a spike of anger at the cold description of the position Expedition Two had found themselves in. Bailey had hit a raw nerve, but she was confident it was not intentional.

Paige smiled before enthusiastically declaring, "I cannot wait to get to grips with the work here. There is so much to do and research to catch up on. I've read everything you sent me including the final papers written by Grace before she died. I'm sure we can get science back on track and where it should be in a matter of months."

Georgia bit her lip, aware that anything she said to defend Grace's suicide would sound like an excuse. Neither Paige nor Bailey seemed to notice.

"Sitting behind Professor Duncan is Lieutenant Charlie Molloy, one of our mission specialists assigned to help with the science research. He'll be working closely under Paige on some technical experiments. He has a PhD in laser physics from Stanford as well as a promising career in the air force."

Molloy waved to confirm who he was but said nothing. Georgia had read his mission file and was intrigued why a military man with his particular expertise had been chosen for this mission. It was a huge investment for someone to simply assist with a number of experiments. He was one to watch for sure.

Bailey continued with the introductions, pointing to the person sitting directly behind him. "This is Doctor Benjamin Coleman, who was supposed to be taking over from Doctor Betts."

Georgia appreciated that Doctor Coleman was a highly regarded physician, originally from Tel Aviv. Much had been made of his Israeli heritage in the press releases. He looked much thinner than his photos and she correctly guessed that he'd not traveled well from Earth. He looked pale and more nervous than his crew mates. Georgia said, "Doctor Betts decided that she liked Mars so much that she wasn't ready to leave when the time came. I know it was a late call but I'm sure the two of you can work out some arrangement to share the load."

Doctor Coleman stared back at her with a blank expression. "If I'd known that, I wouldn't have made the effort of coming here and risking my life. As long as Doctor Betts accepts I'm the senior out of the two of us then I'm sure we'll find a way through this mess."

"I'm not sure that is the case," replied Georgia, looking to Captain Bailey for assistance, but finding none. She continued regardless. "Megan has built up a wealth of knowledge on the effects Mars has on our physiologies. She is now an established specialist, so while she is happy to share that information and work collaboratively with you, I believe she views the relationship as one of equals. But I'm sure you're both professional enough to sort it out without any help from me."

Georgia was unsure if Doctor Coleman's silence was tacit approval or saving his energy for the fight ahead. His face gave nothing away, but she was sure Megan would more than likely be seeking her guidance in the very near future. That was one battle she hoped to stay well clear of.

Chapter 6

Upon return to Alpha Base, Mancuso remotely disconnected the trailer, allowing the MEV's navigation computer to reverse the vehicle delicately onto one of the docking ports located on the front of the facility, allowing the astronauts on board to exit. The two astronauts who'd had the dubious pleasure of riding on the trailer entered the base through a separate airlock at the front of the base.

Doctor Betts and Rashid Qadir were waiting to welcome the newcomers as they entered Alpha Base for the first time and eagerly shook their hands with warm smiles.

Georgia announced to the small gathering, "if you want to store your suits in the room opposite, Megan and Rashid will then escort you to the common room from some refreshments while you wait for the rest of *Lexington*'s crew to arrive. You'll have to excuse the limited selection of drinks available, but we've been waiting for supplies."

Captain Bailey replied, "thanks, we'll do that. But I'd like a quiet word with you first. Is there somewhere we can go?"

"Yes of course. We can go straight up to the control room. It's going to be your new home anyway."

As Megan led the group to the crew common room, Georgia indicated the stairs for Captain Bailey to take. The control room was situated two floors up and, although Bailey managed it in one go, he was breathing heavily by the time they reached the room. He quickly looked around at his new surroundings and sat down in the nearest seat.

"As you can see," said Georgia, allowing Bailey time to recover. "The control room affords a fantastic view across the plain. We completed it only two months ago and I still stand and stare out of this window every day to take in the full experience of being here. Rashid, in particular, has been instrumental to setting up all the equipment here. We can control and monitor all the environmental systems across the base, with sensors and cameras covering all habitable areas. The comms station is over there on the far wall. The console in front of you tracks the power output from the reactor and the solar farm, as well as power consumption. I think you'll find we have everything in hand, but we can show you in more detail once you've had time to settle in."

"Thanks Georgia," replied Bailey. She could see he was dealing with the discomfort and knew it would pass in a couple of days. "You and your team have done an absolutely astounding job. You should all be very proud of your achievements. It makes our lives easier, following in your footsteps. And I am fully aware of the personal sacrifices each of you has had to make."

Georgia shrugged, embarrassed at the unexpected praise. "You do what you have to do," was all she could think to say.

"We're here to take much of that load off your shoulders. You know that one of my duties is to relieve you of command of Alpha Base, and I hope you don't see that as a reflection of your accomplishments. To that end, I would like to transfer that command responsibility now to minimize any confusion. I'm sure you understand."

Georgia had been expecting this moment, but maybe not so soon. She felt as if she wanted to cry but swiftly pushed back that emotion. "Yes Mac, I understand. To be honest, it comes as a relief in many ways. Command was forced on me in unfortunate circumstances and, although I've embraced the opportunity, I've found the responsibility often lonely and stressful. I know I've done the best I can with the resources available to me and am proud to hand over the base to you."

Bailey slowly stood and shook Georgia's hand. "Thank you. I have been carefully thinking about who should be my second in command and I think it should be you. You have the local experience, which is invaluable. I'd be a poor leader if I didn't take advantage of your knowledge. And I've been very impressed by the drive and ingenuity you're demonstrated during your time here. You'll be a tremendous asset to me and the rest of the crew. How do you feel about that?"

She stood open-mouthed for a few moments. "I did not see that coming. I expected Commander Dunn to be your deputy. But I am honored that you have considered me."

"The commander was a potential candidate once Hornet's failure prevented Commander Morgan from getting here. But she doesn't possess your knowledge or passion. I've given the matter a lot of thought on the voyage here, as well as get a second opinion from General Stockton. I'll let you think about it for the next few days. I'm sure you're surprised by my offer."

Georgia smiled. "I don't need to think about it. I'd be honored to take on that role. As long as it allows me to continue working on the robotics program I had planned."

"Absolutely. I'm thrilled that you want to accept the role. We'll make a great team. I'll introduce you to the rest of my senior team later this afternoon and we can start planning out what we want to achieve over the next few weeks. I also want to update you on the situation with Russia and China."

She frowned. "I thought I was receiving all the latest news from General Stockton. We do receive the daily reports on events occurring on Earth, so I am aware of the ongoing tensions with the governments of those countries."

"There are some sensitive issues that haven't been shared because of security concerns. *Lexington* has a state-of-the-art quantum communications system that prevents any possible breaches of security when sharing transmissions with Earth. There are certain highly classified activities that you are currently unaware of. One of the priority jobs here will be to upgrade your comms system to the quantum level. Lieutenant Molloy will be able to assist your chief engineer with that installation."

Georgia wasn't entirely surprised by the revelation. She had long ago realized that news was filtered by NASA in both directions. It made sense that highly sensitive information was not transmitted as it was almost impossible for even the most encrypted systems to be entirely secure. There was no doubt that the Americans were eavesdropping on other countries, so it was to be expected that the same would be done to them. "What do I need to know?" she asked.

"As you're aware, the Chinese are no longer co-operating with the Russians, either here or back on Earth. Tensions have been mounting for some time, but the Chinese have lost patience with their former allies. The Chinese have reached a critical size now and are looking to expand their field of influence. They have been investing vast sums of money in Africa and Australia in return for support for their territory expansions. At this moment, the Chinese Red Army outnumbers the combined armies of Russia, Europe and the USA. It's a scary prospect to think what they are capable of should they ever decide to flex their muscles."

"Yes, I knew most of that. We've seen the Chinese pull out of the joint operations on Mars. We think there are only two Chinese researchers left at the Russian base, Derzost. It's safe to assume they'll relocate once the Chinese establish their own permanent Martian base."

Bailey nodded. "What you may not know is that there are some factions within the Chinese government that are looking towards this planet and seeing an opportunity to extend their sovereignty here. The philosophy is that if Earth is no longer big enough for them, then they'll find an alternative where they can expand their population without hindrance or interference."

"Surely the United Nations wouldn't allow that. And isn't the Moon a more accessible location to start with?"

"You know full well that the Moon has extremely limited resources. Especially when you compare it to what is available here. It's basically a rock in space. The Moon may be strategically important, but it offers no means of building a sustainable community. In any case, the fanatics won't settle for a moon. They want a whole planet. One they can shape into their ideal society from scratch. The most extreme fanatics want to relocate the whole Chinese population within one hundred years."

Georgia was dumbfounded. Sending a mere handful of humans to Mars had come at great expense. The thought of moving two billion people was unimaginable. "That could never happen, so why are we worried about it?"

"You're probably right but it's still being taken seriously by our security analysts. The bottom line is though that we do not understand what the Chinese are up to. The CSS *Shandong* will arrive in Mars orbit in the next twenty-four hours. We know it has at least thirty people on board and there are six support ships. And that's it. They could establish a base in any number of locations. We think it is likely to be near the south pole where there is an ample supply of water, but we won't know for sure until they actually land."

Georgia thought about the problem for a few seconds. "A polar base would be private too. There aren't many satellites that travel over the poles and it would take months to push our existing satellites into a new orbit."

"Precisely. It would be the perfect spot for them to establish a stronghold."

"This isn't what I wanted when I signed up for the Mars program. And it's not what I've been working damned hard for since arriving. Mars shouldn't be an extension of the self-inflicted troubles that are affecting Earth. I hope you're wrong, Mac. We should be focused on creating a planet for everyone as a sign of hope."

"General Stockton advised me you were an idealist. There's nothing wrong with that but I think it unlikely that you or I can change the path of human evolution. History has shown repeatedly that the strongest usually gets what they want by force, whether it be an individual, tribe or nation state. Over just a few thousand years, mankind has managed to fine tune survival of the fittest to become survival of the dominant."

"And where do the Russians fit into all this?"

"We're not sure. There's a power vacuum at the top of their government since President Putin died. They're trying to find their way and, in the meantime, have lost much of their focus. Their ship, *Moskva* also arrives tomorrow and has a crew comprised of scientists and several military personnel. We think their mission is a token gesture to keep up with us. The Russians cannot be seen to be lagging in this particular space race, but they don't have the levels of investment that the US and Chinese have."

"Sound like the next two years will be interesting. I hope you're a good politician, Mac."

Bailey frowned. "It seems as if you're not the only one forced into accepting unexpected positions."

Georgia shook her head. She hoped she and Mac would be able to steer a way through the tricky times ahead. The good news was Mac seemed up to the job, and she was confident he was the best person to lead them forward. Out the corner of her eye, she saw the MEV returning with the next batch of astronauts from *Lexington*. "Thanks for the briefing, sir. But if there's nothing else then I'll head back down to the airlock and welcome the next astronauts. Hopefully, Jackson will be amongst this group."

"He should be," Bailey replied. "And yes, I'm done for now. If you can show me to the crew room, I'll get myself a drink and find you again later." He stood slowly, holding on to the console to keep his balance.

"Follow me," she replied cheerfully.

Chapter 7

Georgia waited alone by the airlock for several minutes, pacing up and down to control the nervous excitement she felt running through her body. The earlier disappointment of not seeing Jackson had been replaced by the eager expectation of being able to greet him properly within the next few seconds.

She heard the outer docking mechanism engage with the MEV and a green light appeared on the wall panel in front of her. She quickly punched in the code to release and open the heavy inner airlock door. Jackson was the first to appear, beaming excitedly as he carried his helmet and a small ornamental box.

"Hey, sis," he called out in his usual laid-back manner, his eyes flashing with joy as he caught sight of her. "Thanks for coming to meet me." He strode forward as Georgia ran to meet him halfway, putting her arms around his waist and holding him tight. They stayed there for several seconds before becoming aware of the other astronauts waiting to exit the MEV.

"Come on," said Georgia, tears of joy streaming down her face. "Let's get you up to the crew room."

Jackson followed into the more spacious corridor and through to the suit room. "Can you hold this?" he said, giving Georgia the box so he could remove his cumbersome spacesuit.

"What is it?" she asked, turning it over and gently shaking it to determine what may be inside.

Jackson smiled at her inquisitiveness. "A surprise."

Georgia glared at him, but it was clear he wasn't going to reveal any more information. He understood she hated surprises, but she was too excited to care too much.

Out of courtesy, she waited for the other six astronauts to remove their spacesuits. While she waited to show them the directions to the crew room, Georgia was amused at how quiet everyone was as they took in their new surroundings. Although there was a complete mock-up of the base back on Earth for training purposes, it couldn't replicate the actual sights, sounds and smells of Alpha Base. Once the astronauts were ready, she led the small party to the common room.

On entering the room, Georgia noticed Molloy and Paige were already deep in conversation with Captain Bailey and Rashid, sharing their initial experiences of Mars and the base. The seven astronauts following Georgia immediately made their way across to their captain, who warmly welcomed each of them with his customary smile and a shake of the hand. In the far corner of the room, Doctor Coleman was speaking with Megan in a very animated fashion. From the pained look on her face, Megan was not enjoying the conversation. Georgia was sure she'd hear the details later but, for now, she wanted some time with Jackson. She discretely led him away to the control room.

Once there, she gave him another long hug, pleased to be able to get closer to him. He hugged her back just as enthusiastically and this time they both cried.

"If only Mum and Dad could see us now," he said pulling away and rubbing the tears from his eyes. "They'd be incredibly proud of us."

She looked up at him and laughed. "Mum would never have imagined in a thousand years that we would both be here on Mars. She thought space flight was a waste of taxpayers' money."

"And Dad would not have allowed his little princess to risk her like on such a reckless mission. Yet here we are. Making history."

Georgia sighed, her eyes still glassy. "I miss them. It would have been nice to prove them wrong. Having my little brother with me here means so much. You don't know how much I've missed you."

"I think the time apart has made you forget how annoying I can be. You'll soon be begging for *Lexington* to take me back to Earth."

"You couldn't be more wrong. My time here has made me appreciate what's most important to me. I'll make sure I spend time to explain what I mean. I'm not the same big sister that waved goodbye to you at Houston twenty-five months ago."

Jackson was intrigued. "Should I be worried? Will Mars have the same effect on me?"

"Don't be silly, Jacko. I've had a personal awakening. I'm sure you're safely immune to what happened to me."

"That's a relief. Do you want your gift now?" Jackson offered the box to Georgia.

"What do you think?" she replied, snatching it from his grasp. She turned it over once, admiring the pattern, before lifting the lid to reveal her mother's jewelry collection. Georgia immediately recognized the gold wedding and engagement ring, a pearl necklace and a personalized silver bracelet. All of them had originally belonged to her great grandmother.

Jackson let her take in the objects. "I know you left them behind intentionally, and I understand why. But the jeweler rightfully belongs to you and should be with you as a reminder of Mum." He rolled his sleeve up. "I'm wearing Dad's watch. It's the next best thing to having them here with us."

"Thank you so much, Jacko. You are so thoughtful. These are perfect mementos and should be here." She carefully removed the bracelet from the box and slipped it onto her wrist, admiring it as the overhead LED lights glinted on the fine scratches. "You are the best brother I could ask for."

"And don't you forget it."

"So, tell me. What are your first impressions of Mars and Alpha Base?"

Jackson raised his eyebrows. "This is a new side to you. You've never asked for my affirmation in the past! You've only shown me a small part of the base so far so it's hard to give a complete opinion, but I'll try. I was lucky enough to sit next to Joe in the MEV so had a clear view of the base as we traveled back from *Lexington*. I admit I was staring up at the cliff face most of the time. Boy, is it imposing! However, I did notice how you've constructed this base across three floors. You can't really miss the regular square walls against the weathered and ancient rock face. The standout component is the huge window which looks as if it came from *Eden*. It's a construction masterpiece."

Georgia listened to her brother with pride. "Sealing the lava tube made an amazing difference, especially once we were able to pressurize the interior. Having the control room on the exterior was a stroke of genius, if I do say so myself. This provides all the functionality and practicality we need for accomplishing our short-term goals."

"Seeing an operational human settlement after the three months traveling through space is a welcome respite as well. Remember when we went on long car journeys when we were kids and we'd watch out for the Golden Arches? Well, seeing Alpha Base had that effect on me today."

"I never know when you're being serious," said Georgia, laughing at her brother's analogy. "There are no Big Mac's or milkshakes here, unless you brought them with you."

"Actually sis, I think there is a pallet on one of the supply ships that contains sponsored burgers, fries and fried chicken. You can only eat them in front of a camera and say how delicious they are."

The thought of junk food after two years of eating processed meals was very tempting but Georgia wasn't going to get too excited until she had it confirmed by a more reliable source. "You realize it's very cruel to lie about food, Jacko" she said.

Jackson seemed to ignore her comment. "You were asking for my opinion. The whole place is far dustier than I expected. Outside and in. It's insidious. Down the edges of this room, the corridors, inside the MEV. It must drive you crazy."

"You get used to it. We tried to keep everything clean but soon found out it's impossible. And we can't afford a cleaner."

"I'll tell you the most surprising thing is there's a strong odor, like a burnt pizza base. And not in a good way. I'd never considered that the planet might have a smell. I've never seen it mentioned I any of your reports. It overpowers the ozone created by your environmental systems. I noticed it as soon as I removed my helmet in the MEV."

"Really? I can't smell anything. I'm sure you won't notice in a few days. Wait until you smell Mancuso's boots when he leaves them outside his quarters! They will leave you with a smell you'll never forget"

"Thanks for the warning. I'll make sure to give his quarters a wide berth. I think I'm going to like it here. I'm sure it has everything I need to allow my geological survey to begin."

"Just let me know if there's anything you need. You'll find it useful to have a sister who's also the newly appointed deputy to Captain Bailey," she said smugly. "As long as you don't take advantage. For now, we should head back to the common room and allow me to greet the rest of your crew. I have so much more to tell you, but it can wait."

Chapter 8

In the early hours of the following morning, as *Lexington*'s slept through their first night at Alpha Base, the Chinese spaceship CSS *Shandong* and its five support vessels entered Martian orbit, two hundred miles above the planet's surface. Despite the complicated and dangerous maneuver, the ships' computers kept a tight formation, less than one mile apart from each other.

On the flight deck, Commander Ding Yaiping stared at the computer screen in front of her, checking the relative position of each of her ships. Her young face revealed no emotion as she scanned the lines of data for any discrepancies that would indicate a fault. The telemetry from each of the craft's transponders was in the green zone across the board.

Colonel Liu Haipeng, sitting next to the commander in the pilot's seat, checked the readout on his navigation computer. Controlling the satisfaction he felt for the precise maneuver he'd completed, he said, "Velocity is within acceptable norms for all supply ships and we are at the correct altitude. All approach systems have worked flawlessly, Commander Ding. We have safely arrived in Mars transition orbit."

"Thank you, Liu. I can confirm your summary. You have completed the task superbly. I will see that you receive a commendation for your professionalism and expertise."

Liu nodded his head in gratitude. He looked at the monitor that showed Mars speeding by below them. The surface was in sunlight and he could see craters and mountain ridges, their shadows offering relief against the lifeless ocher and brown ground. The view was almost mesmerizing and Liu had to tear his attention from the screen. "Have you received any instructions from Beijing for landing?"

Ding looked across at Liu with agitation in his eyes. He was ten years her senior and often seemed to forget she ranked higher than he did. It was a problem she'd continually faced as the youngest commander in the Chinese space force. "I understand your eagerness to take a landing craft to the surface when we are this close to the planet. You need to learn the art of patience, colonel. We will be on Mars for some time and so must choose the perfect landing point. Remember, our base will be the launch point for all future operations here and we need to be absolutely sure."

"I did not wish to pursue the commander on this matter. But after three months, the crew and myself are keen to understand when we will take the next steps on behalf of the Chinese people."

"We will all have our moment of glory, Liu. But remember that I am in charge of this mission and I operate on the direct instructions of the president. We will extend his authority to this planet, in his name."

"Yes captain. I apologize for suggesting otherwise."

***

After several hours sleep, Commander Ding addressed the crew in the ship's galley area, the only space large enough to gather the crew compliment of thirty. Seeing them all together gave her an enormous sense of national pride surge inside her. In her prepared speech, she reminded them that they had supported her as one to complete China's first successful manned mission to Mars. This had been no easy feat and although there remained the process of finding a suitable location to land and establish a colony, it was important to consider how far their space industry had come. The rest of the world would now have to stand up and take notice. The more she spoke, the more difficult it became to control her emotions. She loved her country and the opportunities it had given to her. She thanked each of the crew individually by name, convinced that they also appreciated the deep sense of honor she felt on this momentous day. The Chinese population would be rightly celebrating this achievement and now the country ranked amongst the top space faring nations, without the need to collaborate.

With the resounding cheers of her crew still ringing throughout the ship, Commander Ding returned to her personal quarters to record a message for her superiors in Beijing. General Zhang Zhen's sudden appearance brought her thoughts back to the present. He was a cantankerous military man who had made her life a misery though out the journey. She had lost count of the number of times she'd had to remind him she was commanding this mission. He was a legacy of the old regime though and would soon be consigned to the pages of history. That day could not come soon enough as far as she was concerned.

Without any need for pleasantries, the general demanded, "Now that we're in orbit, I want to take a shuttle across to the *Taipei* to ensure that the experimental device remains undamaged and is ready for use."

Ding shook her head in exasperation. "General. We've been in orbit for less than an hour. There is a long list of tests and measurements to take to ensure that we can break orbit and return to Earth. Those tests are designed for all our safety, and I deem them to be more important than your equipment. Once we have completed those tests, I will consider your request. It will also need to be agreed with mission control. As you're aware, we have limited fuel supplies for each shuttle and their main purpose is as landing craft to ferry astronauts to and from the surface."

The general made it clear he didn't like the response. He stared at Ding, vainly attempting to intimidate her with his piercing eyes. It may have worked on junior officers, but Commander Ding had long since become immune to his bullying tactics. "Exactly how long do you expect me to wait? I have my own orders to comply with and all you ever do is hinder me."

"If you don't like it, take your concerns to mission control. By the time they've received your request and thought about it, we should have completed our evaluation. Assuming we discover no significant problems. Until then, I humbly suggest that you wait patiently for my instruction. I will let you know as soon as you're clear to go."

The general stayed where he was for several moments before turning around and leaving the cabin as quickly as he could.

Ding wondered who she had upset in her career to deserve being stuck with General Zhang on a thirty-month mission. It felt like someone was punishing her. She hoped that his experiments would keep him out of her way for long periods of time. Only then would the mission be bearable.

***

General Zhang struggled to control his anger as he made his way along the center of the ship down to the docking bay. Commander Ding had been a thorn in his side since she had first been selected for the mission nine months ago. The general's initial hopes that he could influence the inexperienced commander had quickly evaporated. She was one of the new breeds of officers who was too scared to use their own initiative for fear it would jeopardize their career. Instead, Ding played it safe. Following orders to the letter and impressing the right people. The general accepted it wasn't entirely her fault; that type of behavior was now actively encouraged by senior officials. He despised them for creating a weak generation of officers and he feared for the future of China as a world power. The country was becoming too soft in its attempts to be accepted in the West as a progressive nation. Its former ruthless streak was being scrubbed from the history books when it should be respected and encouraged.

The general longed for the old days. He'd been proud to serve in the army and had been recognized by his peers and superiors as a fine soldier and a natural leader. His troops had been loyal to him because they saw the fire burning within him while at the same time, he took good care of every one of them. He knew that many would lay down their lives for him if he asked. Commander Ding and the new breed of officers coming through the ranks did not understand blind devotion. That would ultimately be their downfall.

Colonel Liu was waiting for him next to the airlock for shuttle one. "I gather you had no success with the commander."

It was a statement rather than a question. Liu's astuteness was one of the characteristics that had drawn the general to him. "As I feared, the commander remains as inflexible as ever. When time is of the essence, she insists on hiding behind rules and regulations. I should have insisted that she be replaced before we left Earth."

"So, we wait?"

"My patience is limited. We wait for eight hours and then I will assess the situation again. Remain ready for your new orders. For now, follow the commander's instructions. We don't want to raise any unnecessary suspicions."

"Of course, general." Colonel Liu saluted and left the docking bay.

Zhang stayed there for several minutes to recover his composure. If he bumped into the commander any time soon, he feared he may do something he'd regret, and the time wasn't yet right for that. *Soon*, he told himself as he felt the anger inside him subside. The time was close when China would assert itself again and Earth would stand up and take notice.

Chapter 9

Since the Chinese had withdrawn its support for the base it shared with the Russians in the center of Elysium Planitia, the Russians had renamed it 'Derzost', or 'Audacity'. Among the six people who still occupied the camp, two Chinese scientists were waiting for one of *Shandong*'s shuttles to collect them and move them to their new base.

Throughout its lifetime, Derzost had failed to live up to the high expectations of both the Russian and Chinese inhabitants. The life support systems had proved woefully inadequate and had failed on a consistent basis. Rather than carrying out important scientific research, the occupants had found themselves dealing with one potential life-threatening disaster after another. How no one had been killed during that time was a testament to the ingenuity and desperation of the scientists and engineers on the base and back at mission headquarters on Earth.

When it had been time to depart Mars and return to Earth, morale within the base was so low that there had been no shortage of volunteers to take the shuttle back to the Andropov, waiting in orbit for them. Many of the base's inhabitants were malnourished and dehydrated and the enthusiasm with which they had arrived at Mars was but a distant memory. As a result of their weakened state, several Russian scientists were also showing symptoms of kidney failure and other medical conditions. In the end, mission control had to take the unpopular step of ordering a small number of personnel to stay behind.

It was therefore unsurprising that they met the arrival in orbit of *Moskva* and its supply vessels with such excitement. New equipment, food and medical supplies were vitally needed to extend the life of the base and, hopefully, make its occupation more bearable. Fresh blood, in the shape of the twenty-two cosmonauts on board *Moskva* was equally required to bolster the tattered motivation of the long-term residents.

Commander Ivan Koenig had commanded Derzost for the past two years. He dearly wanted to return to Earth but had been given strict and unambiguous instructions to remain. He'd had no option to comply, even though it meant not seeing his family in St Petersburg for another two years. He was in the command center when he received radio confirmation from *Moskva*'s captain, Grigory Stepanov. "Commander Koenig, I am pleased to confirm that we have entered an elliptical Martian orbit. We will be making course corrections over the next six hours to enter standard orbit."

"Congratulations, captain," replied Koenig. "We have been monitoring your orbital trajectories and your presence is most welcome. I look forward to your imminent arrival at Derzost and trust that you have brought some vodka to toast the occasion."

Stepanov laughed. "I promise you that we have plenty of vodka already stored on the landing craft. It is good to see that your priorities have not changed during your time on Mars."

"Some habits are too ingrained to be easily forgotten. I am sure my comrades here feel the same. They have not tasted vodka in over twelve months. Three of our scientists were able to distill some raw alcohol but we couldn't justify the power consumption required. And, in any case, it tasted rancid. Make sure you get here on time."

"You have my commiserations, commander. No Russian should be expected to live in such conditions. If all goes well in our landing attempt, I will be with you shortly after breakfast tomorrow morning. It will be a time for a proper Russian celebration."

***

Commander Koenig meandered along the corridor from the control room to the engineering section. The corridor was dimly lit, the overhead lights flickering as the LED lights struggled to consume the limited power available. Koenig's breath condensed in the cold air and he was glad to be able to put his gloves back on. Siberia was colder, but that did not make him feel any better about his miserable situation.

Chief Engineer Romansky was huddled over the life support console as Koenig walked in the room. Although Romansky had his back to the door and the hood on his coat was covering his head, his small stocky stature gave him away. And no one else dared venture into this section and face the wrath of the irascible chief engineer. Romansky's booted feet shuffled continuously as he concentrated on the screens in front of him and he jumped in surprise when Koenig spoke to him.

"Anatoly, is there any chance of increasing the temperature in here before our new guests arrive? I would like to give them a warm welcome. They are bringing much needed supplies after all."

Romansky replied, "I cannot promise anything, commander. I may be able to divert some power for a short period of time to some areas of the camp. But heating everywhere is out of the question until the new solar panels are delivered and installed. We simply cannot produce enough electricity."

"Is it worthwhile cleaning the solar panels? That has worked in the past."

"You can try although it takes a lot of effort for not much gain. If you can send Alex and the Predatel out to the solar farm for five hours or more, then we should improve efficiency by ten to fifteen percent. I think our two remaining space suits have enough oxygen to complete that duration activity."

"They won't thank me for that, but it sounds like the best plan. And I'm way past trying to be liked. You really should stop referring to Redmayne as a traitor. He has proved his worth over the past two years."

Romansky shrugged. "He has no honor for his own country. I cannot trust a man who does that. At least the exercise will keep them warm and give them something to do for the rest of the day."

***

Alex and Redmayne trudged dejectedly across the Martian surface toward the solar farm located about four hundred yards from Derzost and covering an area equivalent to six soccer pitches. The accumulation of dust on the solar panels was a constant nuisance, especially since the robot built to clean them had failed for the final time ten months earlier.

Redmayne looked at the ground in front of him as he walked, unhappy that he always seemed to get the most unpleasant jobs. He was now an expert on the Russian sewage reclamation system and thought he could clean the air filters blindfolded if he ever needed to. His skills were being wasted, but he had very limited options. He had harbored ambitions to return to Earth on Andropov although he hadn't been surprised when his request was declined. He had been told that it would be embarrassing for the Russians to admit openly that Redmayne had been at their camp as a defector and a murderer. Redmayne understood that, in reality, the Russians simply didn't know what to do with him. And as long as that remained the case, his very existence was tenuous.

"Alex, do you know any of the crew on *Moskva*? And do any of them know about me?"

Without breaking his stride, Alex replied, "I know most of the senior officers from my time training at Star City. Captain Stepanov is a most accomplished cosmonaut. They have decorated him for his achievements on the International Space Station and our lunar research base. Mars is a natural progression for him and I look forward to working closely with him. I am sure he has been fully briefed about you as he will not expect any surprises when he arrives. I do not believe the rest of the crew are aware of your presence. For security reasons it is best that few people know of your existence. We want the Americans to continue to believe that you did not survive your last encounter."

"That must change eventually. I don't want to spend the rest of my time here. It feels more and more like a prison. This is not the reward I was anticipating when you recruited me to assist the Russian space program."

"Maybe not. But I seem to recall that it was you that approached us with an offer of your services. If you had not killed three American astronauts, then you would be on your way to Moscow aboard the Andropov. You have no one but yourself to blame for your reckless behavior. We did not instruct you to be so violent. Plus, you gave us nothing in the end. It reflected very badly on me and has held my career back. But you're not interested in that aspect of your failure."

"But you did train me on explosives and self-defense. You weren't there at the critical time, Alex. I was put under pressure by you to deliver up the Sentinels. I did what I could in the circumstances and have since regretted those deaths. A small amount of luck and the result could have been so different. I'm sure I was close to giving you an alien spacecraft. And then you wouldn't have been able to do enough to thank me."

Alex had heard these excuses many times and was weary of the conversation. Despite the facts, Redmayne continued to refuse to accept responsibility for his actions. "Yet despite those murders, you still failed to discover the Sentinel's craft. I sometimes wonder why you were allowed to return with us when many would have left you on the surface to die."

"That thought crosses my mind every day," sneered Redmayne. "I often wish I'd not been saved. I don't consider my current existence as living!"

"You could always return to Alpha Base. I can ask Commander Koenig to contact them on your behalf if you're not happy here."

"We both know the answer to that one, Alex. The Americans would be only too pleased to hear about my situation here."

"The option has been considered by the crew on several occasions. They have raised the question why we are wasting precious supplies on you when there is barely enough to go around."

Redmayne nodded. "I'm well aware of that. And the fact that some of your comrades call me the 'Predatel'. The 'Traitor'! For what I tried to do on behalf of Russia. I should be called a hero."

"What you did was for your personal gain and not for the benefit of my homeland. Do not try to convince me otherwise. We all know the truth, so there is no point complaining. Let's just focus on the job in hand and maybe we can complete the task quickly."

The pair of them reached the solar farm and began cleaning each of the delicately thin solar panels with handheld compressed air canisters. A short blast of air was highly effective in removing the fine layer of dust that regularly accumulated over the panels, but it was mind numbingly boring work.

The two of them took alternate rows, slowly walking up and down each in silence, careful not to kick up any dust with their boots that would require further work. Occasionally, Redmayne would look up from the panels at his surroundings. From his location, the Russian base looked very simple with several single level buildings covered in soil and joined by interconnecting corridors. It wasn't as large as Alpha Base would now be, or as luxurious.

The control room was easily identified by the three large radio antennas situated on the roof. These allowed for communication with orbiting vessels as well as a direct communication to Earth via a geostationary satellite. There was a weathered and tired feel about the complex with random build ups of dust and numerous tire tracks and footprints. If this was part of Russia's grand plan for colonization of Mars, Redmayne held out little hope of long-term success. Not for the first time, he considered how his life had come to this wretched existence.

A short distance from the camp stood the *Kiev*, the landing craft that acted as a ferry between Mars and any orbiting mother ship. It could also act as a lifeboat in the event of an emergency evacuation of the camp. As such, it was always fueled with enough propellant to get it to orbit. Redmayne took a long look at the craft, knowing that it would be easy for him to pilot it to the *Moskva*. The problem was that they would immediately return him. He was facing a life sentence on Mars with no hope of parole. That didn't stop him from planning and escape though. He told himself that an opportunity would present itself one day and that he must always be prepared. He regarded it as a challenge. In the meantime, whether or not he liked it, he would follow all the orders given to him, including cleaning duties such as this. So, with a deep sigh of resignation, he returned his attention to clearing the never-ending dust.

Chapter 10

By lunchtime, the canteen on Alpha Base was filled with the new arrivals from *Lexington*. After their first night on Mars, the newbies had gradually become accustomed to their new surroundings, some better than others. Many of them had ventured out of the base, taking short walks across the ground in front of the base or traveling further afield using the speeders.

Georgia had not seen Mac that morning. He had commandeered the MEV and left early with two of his crew to inspect the supply ships. She figured it likely that they would be gone all day. Despite their absence, there were sixteen people in the canteen; far more crowded than she had been used to. The atmosphere was different too. She noticed that the room was louder than when it had just been Expedition Two and the conversations seemed more animated. She was ashamed to admit that the last few months had been difficult, with her crew too exhausted to be excited about anything. The arrival of *Lexington's* crew was definitely the lift that she needed.

She spotted Jackson sitting at a table eating lunch with Megan. So, grabbing a bottle of water and a protein bar she went to sit with them. "Hey, are we having fun?" she asked.

Megan's scowl said all she needed to say, but she replied anyway. "Two words. Doctor Coleman! I don't know how or why he was selected but his manner is atrocious. I dread to think how he handles his patients."

"He was brilliant on the journey," said Jackson. "Not that he had much to do other than perform regular medicals and assessments on each of us. He always seemed pleasant and took his time to ensure that we appreciated what he was doing. I think you'll find little complaint from anyone."

"So, you're telling me that it's just me he has an issue with. Or maybe I'm just overreacting to his style."

Georgia said, "I think he's upset that you decided to stay on the planet. He expected to be the chief medical officer on Mars, which I'm sure would have been great for his career. Instead, he finds you here, muscling in on his turf. It's not the clean playing field he wanted. You have more knowledge than him. He's bound to feel slightly threatened. Have you said anything to reassure him?"

"He wouldn't let me speak! He lectured me for nearly half an hour on what support he wanted from me and that I should not do anything without his express approval. The man is a complete control freak. And it's no use smiling at me, Georgia Pyke. You may think I like to be in control, but I am an amateur next to him."

Jackson couldn't restrain himself. "I'm going to enjoy watching the pair of you for the rest of the mission. I didn't think there was much entertainment on Mars. I was clearly mistaken."

Georgia could see how upset Megan really was by the situation. "I can see both sides to this. Megan, I totally respect your reasons for extending your stay on Mars, and I am truly grateful for your ongoing support. You've been the best friend and mentor I could have asked for. Doctor Coleman is a brilliant physician. You know, from your own experiences, what he must have gone through to be selected for Expedition Three. Until two weeks ago he thought he was replacing you. It must be difficult to reset those expectations, so I think you need to make some allowance."

"Yes, I know all that Georgia," Megan was still clearly frustrated. "If he had come in with a different attitude, I would have totally accepted his argument. Instead, he's made it almost personal and attempted to diminish my own worth. I will try to put it down to fatigue on his part, but it's difficult to overcome first impressions. I'll give him another chance but then I'm coming to you and Mac."

"Thank you, Megan. That's all I can ask of you. I'm sure we can make life more pleasant for both of you with just a little effort and compromise."

"I never said anything about compromise! I want Coleman to back down and start acting reasonably and professionally. Then I may allow him access to the medical database."

"Okay. I give up. Try to sort it out as best you can and let me know how it goes."

Megan stood and left without another word. Georgia couldn't recall ever seeing her so angry and upset but wasn't entirely surprised that Doctor Coleman had put her best friend in such a bad mood.

"The joys of command," said Jackson, with a smirk.

"I still don't enjoy the personal side," said Georgia, grimacing. "I can't stay aloof and remote like good leaders can. I get too involved and can usually see both sides to any argument. Why can't people just be reasonable?"

"Like you?"

"Exactly! Life would be so much easier," she laughed. "This is why I'm so grateful that Captain Bailey has assumed command. He can deal with shit like this and probably not lose a minute's sleep."

"He is a very good captain. I've not heard anyone say anything bad about him and he always seems to lead from the front. He will make a great commander. Not that you were a bad commander in any way," Jackson quickly added.

"Is there anyone else I need to be aware of? As the captain has made me his second in command, it would be useful to know if there are any potential flash points or issues I should be across."

Georgia took a large bite of her protein bar and chewed slowly while Jackson gave the matter some thought. "Nothing obvious comes to mind," he said. "The crew are incredibly well balanced and efficient. There were some minor disagreements during the trip from Earth, but they were trivial and dealt with quickly. If I was going to watch out for anyone, then it would be Lieutenant Molloy. He has a quick temper and is very secretive. I had several discussions with him on *Lexington*, but I still don't really know what his main purpose is on the mission. I think it may be military related, but you should confirm with Captain Bailey. The two of them are very close."

"You must be mistaken. I was promised that there would be no military research on Mars. He must be here to do something else but I'm sure the captain will tell me if I ask. What about Professor Duncan? I noticed that you had an eye for her last night at the welcome dinner. I didn't think she was your type."

Georgia could see she'd hit a nerve as she saw Jackson blush. He shook his head and stammered, "I don't know what you mean sis. She's a nice person and extremely good at her job. But I don't think she's interested in a humble geologist like me. She has her eyes on the captain."

"You can't fool me little brother. I've seen that look in your eye before. Be careful. Especially if she really is only interested in the captain. I don't want to see you hurt."

'Don't worry about me. The relationship I have with Paige is purely professional and that will not change."

"I'm glad to hear it. You need to find someone your own age."

"Now you sound like Mum. You do realize there are very limited options to meet single women on Mars anyway?"

"Wait until you return to Earth. Women will be queuing up to date the famous Martian explorer. You'll be so popular that you'll be turning them away. I hate to say it but there's no greater aphrodisiac for women than money, fame and power. Return safely to Earth and you'll have at least two of those."

"That's going to be a long time in the future. Luckily, I have plenty of prospecting to perform to keep me busy on those long, cold Martian nights."

"When do you start? Is there any help you need from me or Mancuso?"

"I need to wait for my equipment to be unloaded. Then I have a pair of drones that I will send out to carry out some spectrography analysis on three interesting rock formations about thirty miles northwest of here. It's very exciting times. If I can locate plentiful mineral deposits, then huge amounts of investment will flow in from mining companies. This could make or break the viability of Alpha as a human colony."

"You're exactly what I've been waiting for," Georgia said with a huge smile. "I still need to tell you the big dreams I have for this planet and being able to trade with Earth is important to my plans."

"One step at a time," Jackson said, grinning at his sister's enthusiasm. "I have big dreams too, but they mainly revolve around making millions on this mission and retiring on an island by the time I'm forty-five. What's the hurry to carry on into the Universe when we still have this planet to discover?"

Georgia looked around the canteen to make sure no one was listening in to their conversation. Even though most of the crew were in the room, they all seemed to be having their own conversations and she was confident none of them were within earshot. Just to be sure though, she leaned across the table toward Jackson and whispered, "I've already encountered intelligent alien life on Mars."

She sat back and watched Jackson's face as he tried to absorb the information. He quickly went from shock to incomprehension as his mouth slowly opened and closed. Georgia continued, keeping her voice low. "It's true. It happened shortly after we landed. The news has been kept classified by mission control and the United Nations. Earth has been under scrutiny for thousands of years by alien races. They've been monitoring humanity's progress and may be still here on Mars, watching us."

"And you decided to wait until now to tell me. Why isn't this public knowledge?"

"I agree that it should be made public. But the World leaders decided that the public isn't ready for this information to be shared. They fear wholesale panic, especially with the conflicts and instability in certain countries."

"I suppose that makes sense," Jackson conceded. "So, tell me about these aliens. What did they look like? Did they experiment on you?" A horrified expression crossed his face. "Were they the ones that insert probes where you don't want them to and suck the blood from cattle? I've seen documentaries about them."

Georgia took a deep breath. *Why did everyone always ask about probes?* "Nothing like that. The aliens I encountered are a species called the Sentinels. They're partly organic and part machine. Humanoid features, about seven feet tall with metallic blue skin. Because they're part machine, they can survive without the need for space suits and can live for thousands of years. But they're just one species amongst many in what they call 'The Confederacy'. I understand it to be a union of countless different civilizations with common beliefs and goals."

"Wow! How many intelligent civilizations are there? Why haven't they revealed themselves to you again?"

"The encounter I had was accidental. They're observation of us is supposed to be passive and discrete. Under their rules, interference in human development is expressly prohibited. In my case, they almost killed me inadvertently and felt a compulsion to rescue me and heal all of my injuries, which were extensive and severe. They took me to their spaceship, which was on a ridge overlooking this base. That should have been the end of it but there were complications when one of our crew was found to be a Russian agent."

Jackson's shocked expression continued as Georgia explained what had happened to her and how some of her colleagues had died. Tears filled her eyes as she recited the details. The pain of those moments came flooding back to her as if they'd only occurred the previous day. The memories were so vivid, particularly the final look on Captain Winter's face. She fought to tell the rest of the story as her brother sat in absolute silence, amazed at what his sister had experienced and not been able to share with him until now.

When she had finished her story, Jackson moved round the table and gave her a brotherly hug, holding her for a long time. By now, the canteen was empty with the crew returning to their assigned tasks. Eventually, Georgia wiped her eyes and looked up at him, smiling. "I wish you could have told me all this before. You're amazing."

"You see now why I have big dreams. I want to see the Universe. I want to experience new planets and alien civilizations that have been around for possibly millions of years. Earth is one small planet and humans are an endangered species unless we can sort ourselves out. The technology that saved my life is probably the tip of the iceberg."

"I can see that. The flaw in your plan seems to be the ability to contact the Sentinels again when they don't want to be discovered. You won't be able to recreate the circumstances from before."

Georgia was feeling liberated at finally talking with Jackson. She had missed being so open with him. "That doesn't stop my desire to give us a chance. At least we know for sure that we're not alone in the Universe. As far as I'm concerned, we now have a definite target to aim for. Something we've never had in the history of mankind. That should be motivation enough."

"If scientists ruled then I'd agree with you. Instead, we have politicians who do not like change and cannot see the bigger picture. You're going to face a lot of inertia, and it's not easy to address when you're so remote. You may not like it, but the answer could be to return to Earth to state your case."

Georgia shook her head. "I'm not ready for that yet. I can do more here by setting an example for the rest of mankind. More people need to be aware of the truth. I really believe that the public is ready to hear this news. The knowledge can be a force for good that brings all nations together for the common good. I know it may take a long time to achieve, but we have to start somewhere."

"Have you really thought this through?" asked a concerned Jackson. "You'll be challenging all the world's religions, head on. They've steadily built their belief systems over thousands of years. People live and die in the name of religion. God, in his many forms, is a source of comfort to billions of people, as is the idea of an afterlife. Do you expect them to simply listen to what you have to say and admit they have been wrong all this time? And what about those countries that have entrenched resentment or hatred against their neighbors?"

"I didn't mention religion," replied Georgia. "The existence of intelligent aliens doesn't preclude the existence of any gods. Who's to say that these new civilizations don't have their own gods, or share gods with our own? Although I'm a non-believer, I'm not dumb enough to challenge the religious institutions. Underlying hatred and suspicion are tougher nuts to crack. It requires strong leadership from politicians. And I think we can use Mars as an example of different nations working together."

"You were right when you told me this planet has changed you. You're not the same person I grew up with. Mars has seen you flourish. I'm sure what you've been through has given you a fresh perspective on life. I sit here in awe of what you want to achieve because it sounds so unbelievable. Yet, listening to you, I'm suddenly convinced that if anyone can pull this off, then it's going to be you. It may be nuts, but you have my full support, whether you were seeking it or not."

Georgia was overcome with emotion. She leaned forward to hug her brother. "Thank you," she whispered.

Chapter 11

Four and a half miles away, in the *Yorktown's* cargo bay, Captain Bailey, Lieutenant Molloy and Professor Duncan were inspecting the remaining equipment pallets containing components for the particle beam weapon.

Although his spacesuit made it difficult, Molloy was crouched on the floor looking at two small cracks in one of the pallets. "It looks like some of the batteries shifted at some point during the journey," he said. "Probably during landing when the ship would have experienced the highest loads. The damage to the casing appears to be superficial but we won't know for sure until we've unloaded and set up."

Bailey glanced above his head at the rows of equipment neatly boxed and stacked and going all the way to the nose of the craft. Most of those containers and racks legitimately contained mining equipment and spares for Alpha Base. The pallets with a red cover, however, were a gift from military special operations and were the key components required by Molloy and Paige.

Bailey's keen eye spotted something unusual on the level above them. "There's some loose cabling up there. Be careful when you unload as it looks as if more than those batteries have moved. I'll report it to mission control because whoever was responsible for loading and securing these supplies did a lousy job. All the equipment here is particularly sensitive. Your mission could already be compromised because of negligence back on Earth."

Molloy agreed. "It's totally unacceptable. Quality control should have triple checked all cargo prior to sealing the cargo bays. I'll let you know immediately if we find any other damage, sir. Let's hope this doesn't set our testing program back. We can't afford any mishaps with *Shandong* and *Moskva* having arrived in orbit this morning. I can only guess that they'll be starting their own weapons testing as soon as they are able to land and establish their firing rigs."

Paige said, "I'll help as much as I can to retain our advantage over the Chinese and Russians. But, if you want to commence testing this week, then we will need some assistance with unloading. While our muscles and nervous systems continue to adapt, I wouldn't feel entirely safe manhandling these bulky pallets."

"Don't worry. I've already lined up Joe Mancuso and Vicky Morris to assist with that," replied Bailey. "They should be arriving here in the next ten minutes. They're the best load masters we have, and of course Joe has a distinct advantage of being stationed here for two years. I'm sure I need not remind you to keep the contents of the pallets secret."

***

Mancuso was teaching Vicky Morris how to operate her speeder. After two years, he was a natural on the Segway type vehicle that allowed astronauts to travel across the Martian landscape. Vicky was a quick learner, however, impressing Mancuso with her skills. They were now both racing at top speed toward the towering *Yorktown*. As they quickly passed the other supply ships, Mancuso was struggling to keep up with her.

"Are you sure you've not done this before?" he asked, unaccustomed to being bettered on the speeders.

She laughed as she replied, "I have to confess that I did practice a lot on the lunar surface. Although the gravity here takes some getting used to, the basic principles are the same."

"I knew it!" declared Mancuso. "There's no way you could beat me after one lesson."

"Oh, and I drive race cars back home too. I don't think I told you that either. It must have slipped my mind."

"I'm going to have to spend more time with you to discover what other secrets you're keeping. It's a good job you're not going anywhere for the next few years." Mancuso was immediately drawn to Vicky, the load master for the *Lexington*. She had an offbeat sense of humor that he could relate to and his instinct told him she would be fun to have around. She was the perfect replacement for Emily Pope.

As they drew closer to *Yorktown*, Mancuso spotted three astronauts descending in the cradle. He was still learning names but recognized Captain Bailey's distinctive gold insignia on the side of his helmet. The cradle touched down on the surface as Mancuso and Vicky stepped off their speeders, fifteen feet away.

"On time as requested, sir," he said, with a salute. Mancuso looked at the two astronauts behind Bailey but could still not remember their names.

"There's no need to be so formal, Mancuso," Bailey replied with a smile. "I run a fairly informal ship and, anyway, it's difficult to salute in a spacesuit. I need you to help Professor Duncan and Lieutenant Molloy with the unloading of some critical mining equipment on *Yorktown*. With so much to unload across the four supply ships, I think there's no time like the present to start the exercise. Vicky is here to learn from you. I'm sure your experiences on Mars have taught you better ways of handling cargo. It can't be the same as the training modules you undertook on the Moon."

The request surprised Mancuso. He had expected to start unloading food and medical supplies for the base. Mining equipment didn't seem to be an urgent requirement when the geologists hadn't commenced their surveys. Training Vicky also seemed unnecessary. She was more than capable of unloading any of the supply ships, if her speeder skills were a good representation of her professional qualifications. But he trusted the captain to know what he was doing. And it was a compliment for the new base commander to recognize his experience so soon. Plus, no one else seemed concerned by the request.

***

As Captain Bailey disappeared literally in a cloud of dust back to Alpha Base on Vicky's speeder, Professor Duncan took it upon herself to take charge. "Joe, you're the only one with experience of unloading equipment on Mars. Is there anything we need to be aware of?"

Mancuso shook his head, "not really. To be honest, it's very similar to how we trained in the simulators back in Florida. I will advise that you take your time. You've been on Mars for only one day and it takes longer than that for your co-ordination to adjust and your body to get used to the effects of gravity. So, safety first and don't over commit. We don't need to unload everything in one day."

"Thanks," replied Paige. "We'll take that advice on board. I was thinking that we have two of us up in the cargo area to load, with the other two here to unload and store the equipment."

"That would have been my suggestion too," said Mancuso. Even though he was the expert amongst the group, it was frustrating being spoken down to by the chief scientist. He put it down to fatigue from the trip but made a mental note to not put up with any more crap. "If you have the manifest, then come with me up to the cargo bay. Molloy can stay here to help Vicky."

Duncan and Molloy glanced briefly at each other as if silently considering Mancuso's direction. For some reason, they looked doubtful, but Mancuso saw Molloy give a small nod before Duncan agreed.

Professor Duncan appeared to relax on the way back up to the cargo bay in the cradle. "What have you enjoyed most about being here?" she asked.

"Just look around," he replied, pointing into the distance. "It's the opportunity to experience what no one else has been lucky enough to do. We are all pioneers. I know the plain looks desolate and unyielding, but I quickly learned from Georgia to see it in a different context. It's a blank canvas that allows us infinite possibilities to explore and progress. You can already see the difference we've made in the past two years and I'm immensely proud to have been involved in that. It's been far harder than I ever expected but that makes it all the more rewarding."

"Wow! I never took you as someone who was so passionate. You do know that there is still enormous interest back on Earth, don't you? Not as much as when you first landed, but the spotlight is still firmly on Mars. Millions of people want to migrate here in the hope of a better life. You'd make a great advocate."

Mancuso laughed. "I don't think we're anywhere close to accepting applications for colonists. We're far from being self-sufficient and it's no place for families or children. It's going to take a long time and an awful lot of luck, but I'll play my part in that as much as I can."

They reached the cargo bay and stepped into the semi-darkness. It reminded Mancuso of unloading the Expedition Two supply ships. The hold had been cleverly stacked full of boxes, pallets, drums, and a myriad of other containers. It was as if someone had played a giant game of Tetris. All of the storage containers numbered or color coded and, in theory, had been packed in a logical sequence for unloading.

Mancuso was quick to notice the damaged pallets. "You've had some slippage during transit. That's to be expected due to the violent forces the ship is subjected to during entry and landing. We had some minor damage but only lost a couple of non-critical items that weren't worth repairing." Pointing up to the levels above them, he added, "That's where you may find more of a mess. The smaller items tend to move around a lot. But if we take our time, I'm sure we can get everything down safely."

Duncan removed the computer tablet from her hip pocket and accessed the manifest, although she understood which items she wanted. "Can we start with those six pallets? The ones with red lids. If we can get those out of the way, it will be easier to access the rest of this level."

Mancuso assessed the pallets' location and agreed. "They don't look too bulky. We can fit two on the cradle at a time." With the help of a small robot porter, the first two pallets were soon loaded and making their way to the surface to be unloaded by Vicky and Molloy. While they waited for the empty cradle to return, Mancuso asked, "Profes-

PAUL RIX

sor Duncan, what's the urgency with this mining equipment? Surely it would be more logical to unpack the rations you've brought with you. I was looking forward to eating something different after all this time."

"It's quite simple. The captain wanted to assess our capabilities after such a long journey," Duncan lied. "Perhaps he thought unloading ration packs would be too easy, compared to the challenge he's set us."

"And you're helping today because...?"

Duncan paused for several seconds. "Because I was available, am suffering no ill effects from the voyage and the captain values my contribution. I don't know why you have a problem with that."

Mancuso didn't expect Duncan to be so defensive. "Calm down, Prof. I was just making conversation. You can't blame me for asking what we're doing the day after you landed. It does seem rather hasty in my experience."

Duncan appeared to relax. "Yes, of course. I'm sorry. I must be more tired than I thought. I didn't mean to get off on the wrong foot with you."

With tension now between them, the two of them worked together in silence for the next minute until the now emptied cradle returned. Mancuso oversaw the loading of the next two pallets, ensuring they were secure before lowering them down to the ground. By now, his temper was back in check.

"Can I call you Paige? I know it can be difficult to transition here after being confined for such a long journey," he said. "Take your time and you'll soon feel at home here. And please let me know if I can help in any way."

Duncan gave a weak smile through her helmet. "Thanks, Joe. I'll do that. I promise you I'm not usually this snappy."

"Don't sweat it. We all have bad days."

Molloy suddenly interrupted their conversation, and Mancuso detected a hint of panic in his voice. "Vicky's had an accident. One of the pallets has burst open and crushed her foot. I think her suit is compromised."

Mancuso leaned out of the cargo door and looked down. He could see Molloy kneeling over Vicky who was laid on the ground writhing in agony. It looked as if one of the pallets had exploded rather than fallen apart, with parts strewn in all directions. "Isolate the leak as quickly as you can, then get her to the MEV where we can assess her injury."

"I can see a small tear in her boot. I think I can patch it," replied Molloy.

With no other way to reach the surface, Mancuso returned the cradle to collect them. As he waited, he watched Molloy and Vicky move slowly to the MEV. A moment later, he heard Vicky's voice over the radio. "I'm okay. There may be some bruising, but I don't think there's anything serious."

"We're still coming down to return you to Alpha for a medical check," said Duncan. "We will have to finish the unloading tomorrow. I'm sure the captain will understand."

"What happened, Vicky?" asked Mancuso.

It was Molloy that answered. "It was a careless accident. The pallet fell as we were unloading it from the cradle. It must have been pressurized as the pallet cracked upon impact. I'll stay behind and clear up and assess what damage there may be to our equipment."

"Is that right, Vicky?" Mancuso persisted.

She avoided his gaze as she slowly nodded. "Yes Joe, it was as Charlie explained. It was a momentary lack of concentration on my part."

Mancuso had his suspicions. Why would simple mining equipment need to be transported in pressurized pallets without adequate warning signs? Although he was no expert, the components he'd briefly seen laying on the ground didn't look like what was listed on the manifest. Something was wrong, but he was positive he wouldn't get the truth from either Molloy or Duncan. The moment wasn't right to challenge either of them. The priority was to return Vicky to Alpha Base for a proper medical assessment.

Chapter 12

Georgia was exercising alone in the gym when Mancuso found her. She found running on the treadmill monotonous and longed to go for a proper run in the open air. But exercise was good for her mental welfare and she had established a daily gym routine to maintain her fitness and positive attitude.

"Can I have a word?" Mancuso asked, as he sat on one of the weight resistance machines.

Georgia pressed the stop button on her treadmill and took a long drink of water from the plastic bottle in front of her. "I hear you had some excitement earlier today," she said, wiping the sheen of sweat from her forehead.

"That's what I want to talk about. There was an accident at the base of *Yorktown*, but I don't think it went down as Molloy explained."

"In what way?"

"The pallet didn't simply split when it dropped onto to Vicky. There must have been a violent rupture to scatter some contents across the ground. Molloy said the pallet was pressurized, but that doesn't make sense if the contents comprised mining components."

Georgia mulled over what Mancuso had just said. "What was Vicky Morris's version of events?"

"She was reluctant to talk as we returned in the MEV, but she basically supported Molloy's account. She seemed nervous, though. I'm not sure if Molloy didn't convince her to agree with him. He had five minutes alone with her before Professor Duncan and I reached the MEV."

"So, you think they're hiding something. That there's a conspiracy?"

"I'm saying they're behaving suspiciously. Everything about unloading *Yorktown* felt wrong today. And, whatever was in that pallet was definitely not mining equipment."

"What would you like me to do?"

"Can you speak with Captain Bailey? He was the one that gave explicit instructions for *Yorktown* to be unloaded. If there is anything unusual going on, he must know. You're his second in command and should be sharing with you."

"Unless he has a good reason for keeping secrets from me. Which would be a very disturbing state of affairs! How is Vicky, by the way?"

"She insisted that Doctor Coleman examine her. I understand from Megan that other than two broken toes and severe bruising of her foot and ankle she's fine. Her boot is repairable and she should be back at work tomorrow."

"That's positive," Georgia replied. They didn't need any more casualties so soon after *Lexington*'s arrival. "I'll talk to Captain Bailey. If nothing else, I'll be able to tell if he's telling the truth or not."

***

Georgia found Captain Bailey reading in his quarters near the control center. She was not surprised that he looked weary after his first full day on Mars. Most of *Lexington*'s crew had already gone to bed and she was sure Bailey would have done too if there weren't so many reports to review.

"Sir, I'm sorry to bother you but have you got a few minutes?"

He put down his tablet and beckoned her into his room, which was still bare as he'd not had a moment to unpack his personal items. "Take a seat, Georgia. What can I do for you?"

Georgia only really understood the direct approach. "It's about the accident at *Yorktown* today. Although Vicky Morris has only minor injuries, Joe Mancuso is concerned that the contents of the pallet did not correspond with the manifest. Are you aware of any discrepancies?"

Bailey stared back, measuring his response. "None that I know of," he replied with a stern expression. "There were some last-minute alterations to the cargo. Perhaps the records were not updated correctly."

"That seems unlikely. There are so many controls in place that everything would have been cross checked before all the hatches were sealed."

Bailey slowly nodded but said nothing, keeping his eyes on Georgia, who continued, "I was wondering about the urgency to remove mining equipment from *Yorktown* when no mining operations are scheduled for months. I would rather have seen replacement equipment and rations shipped to the base first. They're what is desperately needed."

"The decision was mine. There's some very sensitive experimental equipment on *Yorktown*. I was asked to check because they are critically important to all of the corporate investors being able to recover their investments. We're talking billions of dollars at stake. Once those items have been verified to have safely made the journey, then of course we'll be delivering the key items you've rightly identified. It's only a few days' worth of delay. Not that critical."

"Excuse me, but I beg to differ, sir. Having been here for two years, I know what is urgently needed. I thought you appointed me as you second in command for the very reason that I have detailed knowledge and experience of Alpha Base. If you'd consulted with me, I could have advised that spare parts, in particular, are essential in order to get our construction robots and 3D printers operational again to complete the living quarters for the increased population. I feel there's something you're not telling me. How close are we actually working together here?"

Captain Bailey put down the tablet on the desk next to his bed. "Georgia, I think you're overreacting. I've been on Mars for only a couple of days and you have no idea yet how I work or how I manage my team. I appreciate it may take time for the two of us to build an effective working relationship but I'm sure it won't take you long to discover I'm easy to get on with. I expect you to challenge some of my decisions, but

I request that you get to know me first before making too many judgments."

"Thank you, Mac, but if you're looking for my support and trust in your decisions, it's only reasonable that you share your thought processes. But don't take me for a fool. I've been around long enough to know when something isn't quite right. And my instincts are telling me that you're not being upfront about *Yorktown*'s cargo. Or the real reason why Lieutenant Molloy is part of your crew."

Georgia could sense Captain Bailey was weighing up his options. Something about her appeal to his better nature had clearly resonated with him, but he was torn on what he should say next. His response could define their relationship for the foreseeable future. After a few moments, his body relaxed as he resigned himself to sharing the truth. "Okay, point taken," he said. "I should show more trust in you. I think you probably deserve to know the truth. Please know that what I have to tell you is highly confidential. I have been expressly ordered not to share the information with you, but I can see that you're more inquisitive than I gave you credit for. What I tell you next must go no further otherwise we are both in serious trouble. If you want the ultimate test of trust, then this is it. Do you understand?"

Georgia felt a knot in the pit of her stomach. Whatever Bailey was about to tell her couldn't be good news. "Yes, I think so. Although I don't know why I've been kept out of the loop."

"You will by the time I've finished explaining," he replied. "Firstly, I don't think you fully appreciate the effect your encounter with the Sentinels had on world leaders. After the initial shock and consternation that intelligent alien life had been discovered and was observing planet Earth, their feelings changed to fear. They turned to their generals and military advisers to understand what protections were in place to defend their countries against a hostile alien invasion. The answer they received only increased their fear."

"The Sentinels aren't hostile," said Georgia. "They're passive observers only. They've been watching us for thousands of years without any intrusion. Why is our first reaction to think of defense?"

Bailey shrugged. "It's a human condition to protect what is precious to us I suppose. The Sentinels are only one species. How many other alien races are there? And are they all as benign? We just don't know."

"We wouldn't have known about the Sentinels at all if they hadn't saved my life. This is crazy."

"Calm down while I try to explain. "That fear has initiated a new arms race between the major superpowers. Each has spent the past two years designing weapons that could protect humanity. Whether that threat be from aliens or asteroids."

"Or other countries? Fear sounds like an excuse to be creative on how to kill people more efficiently! I don't like where this conversation is heading."

"Whatever your concerns, this is happening. On board *Yorktown* is a developmental particle beam weapon. There has been some testing on Earth, but the scientists need data on how it operates in a vacuum, or near vacuum. With the research to remain secret, the testing couldn't be performed in low Earth orbit or even on the moon."

"You're telling me you've brought a weapon to Mars. Against the strictest UN conventions banning such action." Georgia was outraged that her own government could condone any weapons research on Mars.

"There was little alternative. I promise you that options were considered, but it was impossible to build a large enough facility that could properly test the particle beam. I understand you're angry at only just discovering the truth. The Russians and Chinese have done exactly the same thing and have brought their own weapons. America couldn't take the risk of falling behind in that research?"

"You're kidding me. We've been on Mars for two years and we're already turning it into a military testing ground. If the intention was truly to defend Earth, then why haven't the countries worked together to develop a weapon?"

"That would make sense if it wasn't for the politicians," conceded Captain Bailey. "You'll never get co-operation from all countries when there is a legacy of suspicion and bloodshed. The public is already pressurizing governments to deal with food shortages and climate change."

"The whole idea is ridiculous. Are we really going to fire weapons if an alien race arrives on our doorstep? How effective would those weapons be? We have no idea. Most likely we'd piss off the aliens are they'd annihilate us. Has no one thought this through?"

"I've had troubles accepting it myself, but I've been given my orders. If I'd refused, then NASA and the White House would have found someone else to take my place."

Georgia paused for a moment to gather her thoughts. "Who else in your crew knows?"

"We have restricted the information to Professor Duncan and Lieutenant Molloy as they'll be conducting the testing. We all report directly into General Stockton. Molloy has been closely involved with the development of the technology and is responsible for operating the device."

"So, I'm beginning to understand the urgency," said Georgia. "You want to start testing before the Chinese of Russians so we can brag that we were first."

"Something like that. We're keen to show to the Russians and the Chinese that America leads the way in all space-related activity. If all goes well with testing, there will be a press release stating we have developed and tested the ability to save the planet from asteroids. There will be some opposition around the secrecy of the development program, however the White House will spin the news in such a way that most people will see the benefit to Earth."

"That's a half-truth at best. It's still a weapon that could be used for many purposes if it falls into the wrong hands."

"Would you rather one of our enemies be the first to make that statement?"

"That's my point. We shouldn't have enemies. We should be investing our time and resources for the common good of humanity. Accept that Earth is just one small insignificant puzzle that is the Universe. We're never going to progress if we continue this path of self-destruction."

"I respect your motives. Georgia. But you're not a realist. It will require many generations for people to even start considering what you think is a commonsense approach."

"I disagree. It could happen sooner if we put the trust in people. Inform them of the truth and let them decide."

She immediately saw the look of worry in his eyes. "Now, don't do anything stupid, Georgia. You cannot tell anyone about this. It would be extremely reckless to make any of this public without the proper controls in place."

"More reckless than developing a weapon that's likely to be ineffective against alien technology? Mac, I thought better of you. These weapons will probably lead to our destruction. We should be offering olive branches."

"I don't disagree. Unfortunately, we don't always get a vote. Please, Georgia, I need you to work with me on this. I know it's a huge ask but I would appreciate your support."

"I'll work with you. But I don't support what's being done and will be registering my protect with the general. What's being done here is a huge mistake."

Before Bailey could say anything else, she abruptly stood and left his quarters. Clenching her fists tightly, she marched down the stairs and into the voluminous cavern, her footsteps echoing in the gloom. Swearing to herself at her own stupidity for not anticipating Captain Bailey's news she marched up and down for ten minutes until she was calm enough to return to her own quarters. Unable to speak to anyone, she sat in her quarters, angrily thinking what she could do to prevent the weapons tests from happening without facing a court-martial. She eventually fell asleep with no ideas how she could stop three countries from extending their military presence.

Chapter 13

General Zhang was meditating in his quarters on board *Shandong*. It was something one of his former mentors had taught him early in his career and helped him to remain focused on his priorities. He found meditation extremely comforting when faced with complex situations and it had served him well throughout many years of military service. So much so that he insisted that his senior officers follow his own example. He was aware that all of his officers obeyed him with absolute loyalty and accepted his demands without question, in the hope they would be singled out for further promotion and better postings. And, so far, all of them had been very well rewarded for their devotion.

During the journey to Mars, Zhang had established a daily routine you could set your clock to. Meals and exercise were taken at the same time every day. He ate with the rest of the crew which was highly unusual. Most of his peers chose to eat with fellow senior officials but Zhang had always felt a need to be amongst the lower ranks to show them they weren't forgotten. It was where her had started military service, over fifty years earlier, and it was the common soldier that made the Red Army what it was.

Meditation occurred twice a day, for twenty minutes each time, before breakfast and following the final meal of the day at seven P.M. and it was a brave or stupid person who dared interrupt him during those precious times. Colonel Liu was none of those and waited until the evening meditation session was complete before knocking on the general's cabin door.

"Sir, we have finally completed all the orbital checks. Apologies for the delay but two of the support vessels required course corrections to insert them into the correct orbit."

"I'm not interested in this technicalities Liu. Are you here to inform me that Commander Ding has approved a sortie to *Taipei*?"

Liu shuffled uncomfortably. "No, the commander has yet to receive approval from Earth."

"That is unacceptable," the general rumbled. "I made that request this morning and was assured an immediate response. Send the commander to me now so she can explain herself to me."

***

It was fifteen minutes before Commander Ding appeared in the general's doorway. She looked annoyed at being summonsed although Zhang deliberately chose to ignore it. "I understand from Colonel Liu that you're displeased at my delay to approve your joy ride to *Taipei*."

"It's no fucking joy ride, commander." The general's booming voice was heard throughout the ship. "It's to ensure that the highly delicate equipment on *Taipei* has survived the journey and will perform as designed for this military operation. Your obstruction in that process is entirely unacceptable and intolerable."

Ding wasn't going to be intimidated. "As I instructed Liu, I am waiting for clearance. If you are not happy with the process, then I recommend you make an appeal to Beijing, as you have done on countless other occasions when trying to undermine my authority."

"If you were not so ineffectual, I would not need to seek out the real decision makers. You should develop a backbone and make command decisions. That's what commanders do."

"With respect, General Zhang, you're an ancient relic that should have been put out to retire years ago instead of living off past glories. I do not need to take advice from you."

The general grinned, revealing his missing and rotting teeth. "That is another of your failings, commander. Many of my former officers are higher in the ranks than you could ever possibly dream because they recognized my wisdom. I will speak to Beijing, but you should know that when the outcome is in my favor, it won't look good on your record. Can you ensure that a shuttle and pilot are ready to depart once confirmation is received? Dismissed."

Commander Ding hastily disappeared as the general chuckled to himself. He knew that she would be seething after their latest confrontation. The arguments were the only part of their strained relationship that he relished. It was a shame that she was not a more worthy adversary.

***

While Zhang awaited the response from Beijing to his request, he visited the galley for a drink of hot water. It was all he ever drank except for special occasions when he would have one glass of baijiu. He returned the salutes he received from the four crew members already in the room, filled his pouch with hot water and floated up to the flight deck for a view of Mars.

The planet racing by below looked desolate and unforgiving. But it was a prize worth fighting for. There was potential in the form of water ice and minerals. More than enough for the Chinese people to expand and flourish. For too long had his country been constrained and bullied by the Western powers. Despite having the largest population, his people had made one compromise after another to accommodate western sensibilities, each time eroding their own culture and heritage. The Chinese should be proud and take their rightful place. The Americans, Russians and Europeans should rightfully be the ones making compromises to China. Those countries had long forgotten the values and ideals that the ancient Chinese philosophers had introduced to the world. And worst of all, his country's leaders had watched and allowed it to happen. He would never understand how that had occurred. Those leaders should be ashamed and punished.

He was aware that Colonel Liu had joined him. "Are you admiring our new home, general?"

Zhang looked around to check that they were alone. He took a sip of his water and quietly replied, "It may look bleak now but one day it will be a lush world, a perfect location for our republic. My only regret is that I am too old to see how it will look. It is reassuring to know that there are strong people such as yourself who have the vision and capability to see this venture through."

"There are many of us that have your beliefs. We've all experienced the imperialists in the West prevent our expansion plans and punish our trade. They are happy to see our people starve rather than allow us to thrive as they do. We are eager to follow the daring example you are setting."

Zhang smiled, knowing that he had been right to select Colonel Liu as his deputy and, ultimately, his successor. There were several candidates on board, but the colonel was clearly superior to any of them, and his loyalty over the past twenty years had been exemplary. Liu was a natural leader, unlike Commander Ding, and there was no doubt that the men would follow him.

"We will transfer to *Taipei* in the morning to confirm the functionality of our weapons system. I am awaiting confirmation from Beijing and am confident they will provide the answer I seek overnight. Commander Ding's petty inadequacies will not delay us anymore."

"That is good to hear, general. It has been a long journey to get to this point and we are ready for action. Personally, I am enthusiastic to witness the weapon in operation. If it can do half of what the scientists tell us, it will be an incredible experience to see it in action."

Zhang wasn't sure if Liu was referring to the journey to Mars or the time since Liu had first been recruited to the cause many years earlier. Liu was correct in both instances, and Zhang could understand the colonel's excitement that the plan was finally reaching its conclusion. He realized he had been extremely fortunate that the discovery of extra-terrestrial life on Mars had accelerated the technology development he required. For too long he had feared he would die of old age before his dreams came to fruition. He had seen too many of his fellow generals wither and die and it was only his dogged determination that had sustained him. Now, the culmination of years of meticulous planning was within his grasp. There was nothing standing in his way.

"What is the latest on the American and Russian missions, Liu?" He didn't expect either country to be as advanced in their planning as he was, but there was no point in taking anything for granted.

"The Russian vessels have corrected their orbit as anticipated. They will be in the correct inclination to make a landing attempt at their base early tomorrow morning, around six A.M. As for the Americans, our satellite has detected some activity on the surface near to their base. As it only their first full day on Mars, it is unlikely they have considered unloading their weapon."

"Have you established the location of the American's ship that brought their particle beam?"

"Yes sir," Liu replied, with more than a hint of pride. "The satellite was able to take images from an angle that allowed us to read the name *Yorktown* on the side of the ship. We have its exact location plotted."

"You have done good work, Liu." Zhang clapped the colonel on the shoulder in thanks. "Now, we should get some rest. Tomorrow is going to be an important day for our country that will be celebrated for eternity."

Chapter 14

Georgia had a fitful night's sleep. The frustration and anger she felt not subside. She had been duped by the men she was supposed to trust, General Stockton and Captain Bailey. The surprise disclosure filled her with misgivings. She had naively believed Mars was always going to be a peaceful colony where different nations could work in harmony to create a better world. She'd never expected it to be perfect. There were qualms around the commercial exploitation of the planet and the risk that the wealthier nations would take more than their fair share, but she could justify that in exchange for funding of the exploration of Mars. And there was always the hope that the UN would be able to put some controls in place.

Bringing weapons to the planet was a whole new ball game. There was a distinct danger of repeating the conflicts that were happening back home. Let alone the vast sums of money that could be better spent. If this was really how human colonization was going to be, moving from one planet to another with larger more powerful weapons of destruction, then she wanted nothing to do with it. She had considered resigning her post with immediate effect but, in the end, decided to give it a few days.

At breakfast she found Mancuso sitting alone reading a message on his tablet computer while enthusiastically eating an omelet. He looked up at her and said, "I hope *Lexington* brought more of these. There are less than twenty omelets left in the stores and I always like to start my day with eggs, even if they were cooked years ago. You look concerned. What's on your mind?"

She sat down opposite him. "I spoke with Mac last night. You were right to be suspicious about the equipment on *Yorktown*. I can't tell you what it is but, in my opinion, it has no right being here on Mars."

"What are you going to do?"

"I'm going out to *Yorktown* this morning to take a closer look. Try to look surprised when I rock up. I want to speak with Professor Duncan and discover what she plans to do with the equipment so that I can determine if it poses a risk to Alpha Base."

"With Molloy's military background I can make a good guess at the type of device," whispered Mancuso. "Even if it is a weapon of some kind, Stockton must have passed it safe for the mission. It must have taken up a lot of critical mass on take-off."

"I can't confirm that Joe. I don't like being blindsided like this. Especially by General Stockton. What else haven't I been told?"

"Let's wait to see what you discover today then."

***

Georgia arrived at *Yorktown* at eleven A.M. on a speeder. By that time, the unloading was in full flow, with eight pallets stacked neatly next to one of the landing supports. The cradle was descending with two more bright white containers. She noticed Molloy and Vicky watching her as she pulled up and dismounted. Their spacesuits were pristine compared to her own.

Walking up to them she asked, "how are you feeling today, Vicky? Is your foot in much pain?"

"It's badly bruised but the painkillers help, Miss Pyke. It was a careless accident. I forgot what gravity can do."

"Please, call me Georgia. Everyone else does. It can take several days to get used to life back on the ground. Three months in space does strange things to the mind as well as the body. I'm glad to see you're up and about today. How are you progressing?"

"Much better today. There's only one more load after this one, and then we can move on to the other supply ships."

It fascinated Georgia how quickly the *Lexington* crew were adapting to life on Mars. *NASA's doctors and dieticians must be learning how to counteract the negative effects of the three-month transit time from Earth.* "Lieutenant Molloy. Was any of the equipment damaged?"

Molloy appeared reluctant to answer but was in no position to refuse to answer questions from the second in command. "It's hard to tell until we put all the components together. The contents of the pallets were carefully packed and cushioned to protect them against any sudden impacts. I carried out a brief visual inspection yesterday and everything appeared to be in order."

The cradle touched down on the surface several yards behind Molloy. "I'll move out of your way while you unload," she said. Georgia watched as Vicky and Molloy efficiently controlled one of the robotic tractors to move a pallet and stack it with the others, before repeating the exercise with the second pallet.

Just as Vicky was set to send the cradle back up to the cargo bay, Georgia said, "I'll jump on board. I'd like to take a closer look at the remaining cargo." She climbed onto the cradle without waiting for an answer and began the steady climb. From her vantage point, she could see all the ships that had landed on Mars, the solar farm, Alpha Base and the skeletal frame of *Eden's* wreckage that they had cannibalized for parts. The view was a cross between a space port and a scrap yard. Either way, it blended in well with the desolate bleakness of Hellas Planitia.

She was welcomed to the cargo bay by Mancuso who had spotted her arrival on the speeder. "Good morning Georgia," he said. "This is a pleasant surprise. Have you come to check on our progress?"

Georgia restrained a smile at Mancuso's bad acting. "Yes, particularly following Vicky's accident yesterday. I wanted to ensure that the unloading wasn't being rushed unnecessarily."

Professor Duncan replied, "I can assure you that everything is under control. Isn't that correct, Joe?"

Mancuso nodded in agreement. "It has been far smoother today. We have only one more pallet to unload from here and we've had no further mishaps."

Georgia turned to face Duncan. "Paige, I don't think Mac properly introduced us yesterday. I'd like a few moments of your time now just to get to know you better. I'm sure Joe can manage the final pallet on his own."

Duncan switched her comms channel to private two-way so that no one else could hear their conversation. "I was waiting for you to speak with me. Mac told me he'd had to share the news of our research with you and that you had several concerns. What do you want to know?"

"I'd like to know what tests you intend to perform. Is there any danger to the base or the crew? What happens after you complete testing?"

"Georgia, first let me tell you that I always believed it was a mistake not to keep you informed. But the need for absolute secrecy meant it was impossible to tell you in advance."

Georgia shook her head. "I don't quite understand that. Who is it a secret from? You know that the Chinese and Russians have brought their own weapons to test and they no doubt know what you're doing here. It seems to be a very open secret already. Who doesn't know what's going on?"

"The public. There would be mass outrage and panic if this was to make its way into the press. It's not the first time that weapons development has been kept confidential. Successive governments have run covert development since the first world war. Plus, there's the added complication of the Sentinels and other extra-terrestrials."

The answer didn't convince Georgia and she decided on a new approach. "So, what exactly is the equipment you are testing?"

Professor Duncan appeared to relax at this question and smiled as she was able to share some technical information. "We've developed a linear particle accelerator that accelerates charged ions to a high speed by subjecting them to a series of oscillating electrical potentials along a linear beam line. In our first series of experiments, we'll be using the particle accelerator to speed up positively charged hydrogen ions until their velocity approaches the speed of light. The resulting high energy protons will capture electrons from eight electron emitter electrodes to create an electrically neutral beam of high energy hydrogen atoms."

"I only understand a small part of what you just told me, but it sounds like it requires a lot of energy."

"You're right, it does. But in the final few months prior to leaving Earth, we had a breakthrough and improved energy conservation by more than sixty percent. It's far from being perfect, but the pulsed particle beam emitted by such a weapon will contain five gigajoules of kinetic energy, maybe more. The speed of the beam, in combination with the energy created by the weapon, will make it virtually impossible to defend a target against the beam. Even shielding or materials selection would be ineffective, especially if we're able to maintain the beam at full power and precisely focused on the target."

"What exactly is your target going to be?"

"Whatever we want it to be. An alien invasion fleet. An incoming asteroid, assuming we can maintain full power for long enough."

"Other countries on Earth? I can imagine the army can see great potential in space-borne particle beams."

"Georgia, I know you're not happy about this but try to understand. Yes, this weapon could be used on Earth. I know that. But it's less discriminatory than any other weapon in our arsenal. It's far more like a surgeon's scalpel as it can be accurately and narrowly targeted. The particle beam is nothing like nuclear warheads, grenades or even bullets. It's a precision tool that can be defensive as well as offensive."

"Depending on who's in control," interrupted Georgia. "I appreciate this is your pet project, Paige, but my unbiased view has so many concerns. Are the Chinese and Russian weapons similar to yours?"

Professor Duncan nodded. "We believe so. Directed energy weapons are the logical next step. There are several ways that such a weapon can be designed and used but they're all variations on a theme."

"So, tell me Professor, what would happen if either country targeted their particle beam at this base?"

"That's not going to happen," Duncan replied confidently. "Firstly, that would be a declaration of war that would find its way all the way back to Earth. There would be international condemnation. But secondly, and more importantly, it's not technically feasible. The technology developed to date is ground based only. Whoever fires the weapon needs a clear line of sight on the target. The bases are too far apart. It's not possible for any country to see the other's base from their own location."

"Humor me for a moment," said Georgia, now staring intently at the professor. "Both the Russians and Chinese have ships in orbit. If they target this base from space, what would be the consequences for us? How difficult would it be to prove there had been an attack rather than a catastrophic accident?"

Professor Duncan thought about it for several moments. "Okay, this is purely hypothetical to answer your specific question. Assuming that the ships have sufficient power reserves and an accurate targeting system that can compensate for their ship's orbital velocity a five second burst of a particle beam could punch a hole through that nice shiny window you have in your control room. That would cause an explosive decompression that would destroy the front facade of Alpha Base. I don't know how strong the internal seals are, but anyone in the cave area may survive. Everyone in the control center, crew room would stand no chance."

"As I thought," said Georgia. "Communications would be destroyed, and any survivors trapped inside the cave with no means of escape. In the meantime, the Chinese and Russians deny any knowledge and instead offer their condolences."

"But the odds of it happening are infinitesimally small. As I explained, there are several extremely complex technical issues to overcome to make that scenario even remotely likely. And surely your fears make it even more important that we develop our own weaponry to counter such an attack."

"You're missing my point. There will be strategists amongst the Russians and Chinese who will justify their programs because of the fear of what we may do to them! You should have all been better spent dissuading each other to bring these weapons to Mars, or even creating them in the first place. You've made this a far more dangerous place than it already was."

"I disagree. I intend to pursue the research with the skillful assistance of Lieutenant Molloy. You're more than welcome to observe and ask any questions. If you have any more worries, I suggest you raise them with the captain or General Stockton. For now, I need to get back to work." Professor Duncan headed back to where Mancuso was standing as he lowered the last pallet to the ground.

Georgia stayed where she was, looking around at the mountains of equipment that was waiting to be offloaded in the coming months. It was staggering how much mass had been transported to Mars. But that knowledge held no comfort for her. How could no one else see the inherent danger they were now placed in? It was bad enough not knowing what was happening at Alpha Base without contemplating what may be occurring on other parts of Mars or even in orbit. She involuntarily shivered at the thought of how vulnerable the base now was. She wondered if this was how her grandparents had felt when Sputnik launched in 1957.

Chapter 15

The Russian landing craft, *Tolstoy*, landed softly on the newly cleared landing pad a short distance from Derzost at shortly before seven A.M, kicking up a cloud of dust and small rocks which quickly settled. Its modern, clean looks contrasted sharply with the older *Kiev* that was battered and dented after two years of rough service. The sun was just rising above the horizon, its weak light reflecting off the cockpit windows. There was a huge cheer within the Russian base as they watched the successful landing.

Tom Redmayne was less animated than the Russians. He had nothing to celebrate and appreciated that he would be excluded from the drunken party that was likely to take place that evening. If he was lucky, he may be offered one glass of vodka from Alex, but he wasn't holding out any hopes. The longer he remained at the Russian base, the more he realized that they did not want him there. His presence was a potential embarrassment. How long would it be before they arranged for him to disappear permanently? He wasn't sure, but it was the only logical conclusion. He had to find a way to escape.

Because returning to Alpha Base was not an option, Redmayne had approached the two resident Chinese scientists to determine if it was possible, they would take him to their new base. Initially they had chosen to misinterpret his requests. However, it soon became clear that even the Chinese would not accept him or his considerable expertise. His history was a recurring blot. No one wanted a traitor and a murderer, whatever other skills they may have to offer. Although he understood peoples' misgivings, it didn't make the rejections any easier and only increased his sense of desperation.

This was a new experience for him. He had always been self-sufficient. Growing up in South Africa, his father had taught him from an early age not to rely on anyone but himself. People always let you down, his father had told him. And his father was right. He'd experienced various friends and colleagues not following through on promises for jobs or research grants. The fact that he always had contingency plans was a testament to the tough love his father had shown him. On safaris he had always taken excess provisions, bullets and knives despite the looks of derision from his fellow hunters. "Why are you carrying excess weight? You will tire and hold us back," they had told him. Yet on the one occasion when the jeep had crashed, damaging the radio equipment, he and his companions would surely have died without his additional supplies.

Mars was an entirely different proposition. It was a prison rather than a game reserve, with no obvious means of escape. Survival meant staying close to his enemies in the hope that they saw some value in his ongoing presence. While Redmayne was confident that he was the smartest person on the base, his superior intelligence meant nothing when he was outnumbered.

***

Redmayne watched through one of Derzost's viewing windows as seven cosmonauts disembarked from the *Tolstoy*, walking carefully down a flight of steps to the surface. They lowered an open topped vehicle from the underside of the shuttlecraft, together with two medium-sized crates. Once the crates were loaded onto the vehicle, four of the cosmonauts clambered aboard and drove toward the base while the remaining cosmonauts started the short journey on foot.

"You don't look very pleased at the arrival of our new friends."

Redmayne turned to see Alex was also watching what was occurring outside. "I have no feelings either way," Redmayne lied. "Although it is always good to welcome new faces."

"You're right, of course. And, more importantly, they are bringing urgently needed supplies. We must frustrate even you at the emergency rations we have been eating for the past two months."

Redmayne grimaced. Whoever had designed those rations must either have had no sense of taste or expected that no one would ever be required to eat them. They were foul and, although there were supposed to be five different flavors, they all tasted the same; rancid cabbage and some other unrecognizable vegetable. "A burger would make a nice change," he muttered.

Alex grinned. "Ah, with fries and a shake? I entirely agree my friend. I doubt our nutritionists in Star City had the same thoughts, but they may surprise us on this occasion."

"I'm not holding out any hopes other than they took into account some of my dietary requests. Even a condemned man gets to choose his last meal."

"You should not talk like that my friend. You have many uses. You may think the commander is tough on you, but he has plans to utilize your expertise. Some of the experimental equipment being delivered would benefit from your experience when it comes to conducting experiments."

Alex's revelation lifted Redmayne's spirits. "When were you going to share that news with me? And what types of experiment will be carried out?"

"I cannot give you more information at the moment. The commander will speak with you when the time is right. As for the experiments, let me just say that your experiences before joining us were a huge benefit to the design and need for the equipment being delivered from Moscow. The equipment is vital to Russia's national security. If the experiments yield the expected results, and they see you have been actively involved, it may well improve your chances of returning to Earth"

Redmayne was intrigued and looked quizzically at Alex hoping to discover more clues. This was a game that Alex played sometimes. Dangling half stories and random facts to tantalize and torment him. But he'd learned that Alex would not reveal any further information, however much he pleaded or demanded. It was not a game that Redmayne enjoyed, and he refused to play it this time. He would wait for the commander to share the details. It was good to know that he would soon be carrying out some scientific work again soon though.

***

Twenty minutes later, Redmayne lined up with the rest of Commander Koenig's crew to greet Captain Stepanov and his cosmonauts. Stepanov was the first man to step out of the airlock. He was over six feet tall with chiseled features and short blond hair. He gave the commander a big smile before they warmly embraced. Only then did Redmayne spot the bottle of vodka in the captain's right hand.

"It is good to see you again, my friend," said Stepanov, stepping back from Koenig. "It is traditional for a stranger to bring a gift to a new home, so I present you with this finest Beluga vodka."

"You are no stranger, Grigory. But I accept your gift. You are most welcome at Derzost." Commander Koenig clapped Stepanov on the shoulder and took the bottle offered to him. He then introduced the captain to each of his crew before finally reaching Redmayne.

"So, this is the infamous Predatel," sneered Stepanov as he stared closely at Redmayne. "You are bigger and stronger than I was expecting. For some reason, I thought you would be small and weaselly."

Redmayne didn't flinch at the insults. He knew he was being tested and any reaction would only lead to further insults and possible physical injury. Instead, he said, "It is good to meet you finally, Captain Stepanov. I have heard many good things about you."

"I wish I could say the same thing. But they have told me that you have certain qualities that may be useful to our mission. You will be working with Professor Kozlovsky and reporting to me over the next few months. I trust that you will not disappoint me too much."

Redmayne continued to hold his gaze. "I am sure you will be more than satisfied with my work, captain."

"We'll see." And with that, Commander Koenig ushered Captain Stepanov toward his quarters for a private conversation. It was left to Alex to introduce the rest of *Moskva*'s crew as they stepped wearily from the airlock, one by one. Each of them gave Redmayne a look of disdain but, by now, he was beyond caring.

The last person to exit the airlock and be introduced to the crew was Professor Anna Kozlovsky, who was in her early forties and looked too elegant amongst the other cosmonauts who had just arrived. Any misgivings he had about working for a strange Russian scientist were immediately forgotten. He smiled and held out his hand as Alex introduced him. "Hello Professor, I understand we will be working together."

She coldly refused to take his hand and said, "not exactly, Mister Redmayne. You will be working for me and will follow my instructions to the letter. I have some delicate and important experiments, and I do not want someone like you to screw it up. Is that clear?"

Her cold blue eyes made it clear she meant business. Redmayne felt that she must be highly regarded in whatever field she worked in and was confident that he would be able to change her opinion of him once he demonstrated his own skills. Still smiling, he replied, "perfectly. When do we start?"

"As soon as the equipment is transported from *Moskva*, which is scheduled for tomorrow. I will brief you later today on what I expect from you and the tasks that you have been assigned. For now, I would be grateful if you could collect my personal belongings from the airlock and take them to my quarters." Without another word, she followed Alex into the base for a guided tour.

Redmayne followed her with his eyes, not sure what his first impressions of her were. She was not what he normally expected of a mission scientist. But then, he still didn't know what experiments she was going to be conducting, and he only had Grace Cooke to compare her against. Romansky nudged him sharply with his elbow as he walked past. "Congratulations, Predatel. It looks like they have promoted you to errand boy!"

"Fuck you!" replied Redmayne angrily, but all he got in response was a mocking laugh from the surly chief engineer who carried on walking.

Chapter 16

General Zhang was in a furious mood. Overnight, he'd received a response to his request, and it was not the answer he wanted or expected. The gutless fools in Beijing had instructed him to continue with the original mission profile. He was to wait until after they had landed and established a base on Mars. He banged his fist on the wall of his cabin three times in anger. Although he understood fifteen minutes of meditation would calm him, he wanted the burning rage to continue.

One minute later, Commander Ding made the mistake of poking her head through the hatch to his quarters with a smug look on her face. "Are you okay general? You look as if you've had some bad news."

The general glared back at her. "You know full well that my request has been declined. You must be very pleased with yourself. I cannot believe those mindless idiots in control of this mission have refused me. Don't they see how critical it is to our progress?"

"Perhaps you are losing your power, old man. They have seen that you are not supporting China's mission as you should. A good general should know how to follow orders as well as give them."

"I don't need a lecture from you, commander. This is not over, and I will get my way. The weapons testing is critical to our success. We must know that the particle beam works before the Americans or Russians prove their own technologies. I will not allow it to be delayed any longer."

"You'll do no such thing. You have been given clear instructions by me and also by your masters in Beijing. You have tried to undermine me for the last time. A shuttle is being prepared, but it will take our people to the surface of Mars. We will establish a base near the South Pole to allow us a plentiful amount of water. Only once the base is secure and operational will you commence your weapons program. You can either stay here on *Shandong* or join us on the planet. The choice is entirely yours. I trust there is no confusion in what you have to do."

As he listened to Commander Ding, the general regained control of his emotions, becoming calm again. In a low voice he said, "thank you commander for clarifying my options. There is no longer any confusion in what I must do."

Ding nodded. "Thank you, general. That is reassuring to hear. I look forward to seeing you in the briefing area in one hour. I will be allocating tasks for the landing party."

***

Zhang was the last to arrive in the briefing area. He quickly looked around the room to note who else was present and was gratified to see the faces he wanted around him. Commander Ding looked impatiently at him. "Thank you for joining us, General Zhang. Now we can begin. My intention is to launch a shuttle at two P.M today. If we miss that launch window, then we will not be in the correct inclination for the landing zone for another eighteen hours. Colonel Liu, is there any reason to prevent launch at that time?"

Liu looked nervously at the commander before directing his gaze to Zhang. "I think you should speak with the general about that," he said.

Ding was momentarily surprised by Liu's answer. "And why is that?"

Zhang leaned slowly forward and said, "because we're not going to Mars yet. The shuttle will launch this afternoon, but it will take me across to *Taipei*. I will have the opportunity that I have demanded."

A flash of anger crossed Ding's face. "How dare you speak to me like that. I made it clear to you this morning that you will follow orders. Not just from me but also from Beijing." Her face was red with outrage at the general's latest attempt to undermine her. She looked at the others in the room and added. "To let you all know, General Zhang has repeatedly requested a shuttle to *Taipei*, and I have refused him. He requested permission directly from Beijing and they have also refused him. I don't know what game he thinks he is playing but we are going directly to Mars."

Colonel Liu replied, "we know what the orders are, commander. But we follow General Zhang. As he just said, his instructions are that Mars can wait until we have tested the particle beam weaponry on *Taipei*."

"That's mutiny! You and the general cannot hope to make that work. You will face a court martial and be executed when we return to Earth. That will be an inglorious end to your careers." Ding looked to the others in the room. "Can I have two volunteers to escort these treasonous cowards to their quarters while I decide what to do with them."

Only one person moved forward. But as soon as he noticed that no one else in the room had moved, he nervously returned to his position and avoided direct eye contact with anyone.

Ding spun round to face Zhang who was smiling at her in triumph. "You appear to be outnumbered, commander. Most of the ship's crew are loyal to me. They were selected because they're either my officers or have been recruited by my former officers. Believe me, I hoped it wouldn't come to this. If you'd accepted my request, then I could have avoided this unpleasantness. Instead, I'm now assuming full control of this ship and the mission."

Ding's shoulders slumped as she realized the futility of her position. "How can you hope to get away with this without support from Beijing? You've now condemned everyone on this ship to execution when they return to Earth. I hope that you're the last one to face the firing squad. You should be made to watch your officers die one at a time because of their misplaced loyalty to you. I look forward to seeing it happen at first hand."

"Brave words, commander. Unfortunately, you won't have the opportunity to see my death. In any event, we will return as national heroes once we have completed our mission and restored China's pride."

"That's insane. Not everyone on *Shandong* is loyal to you. I doubt they will blindly switch their allegiance."

Zhang laughed again. "One thing I've learned in my long career as a soldier is not to underestimate the power of survival. It's a core part of everyone and will make people do amazing things that they didn't know they were capable of. Survival can affect them physically and alter their beliefs. After all, who wants to die for a noble yet hopeless cause?"

"So, you'll threaten everyone with death unless they support you. Is that how you establish your loyalty and devotion? It's barbaric."

"No commander. It's far simpler than that. I set an example that others can learn from. It's an education process." Zhang nodded to Colonel Liu and the officer standing next to him. Before Commander Ding could react, she was grabbed roughly by both arms. She fought to release herself from their grip, but the two men were larger and more powerful.

"What happens to me now, general? I will not become one of your lapdogs. Your threats won't work."

"I realized that a long time ago," Zhang replied casually. "You're going to be the example I set for everyone on board to see."

Before she could react, they quickly took Ding from the briefing area to the emergency airlock and placed inside. Zhang closed the door and keyed the controls to make sure it was sealed before looking through the glass window at Ding who still looked shocked and confused by what had just happened. The full extent of her plight still hadn't dawned on her. She keyed the comms button. "You can't keep me here forever, Zhang. Beijing will be expecting my report later today. How are you going to explain my absence?"

"A tragic accident for such a promising young officer. Your space suit failed while you were inspecting the exterior of the ship, and we were unable to save you," replied Zhang, with a look of pure evil. "No one here will dispute the events so the gullible idiots Beijing will have to accept my account. Don't worry, I'll include a recommendation for a posthumous award."

For the first time, Zhang saw the look of pure terror on Ding's face as she finally registered what was about to happen to her. It was an expression he had seen many times before and had long since become immune to any feelings of sympathy, particularly where the death was necessary for an important cause.

"No!" she screamed. "You can't do this. Someone stop him. Please!"

As he expected, nobody behind Zhang moved. Having heard enough of her desperate cries, he turned off the intercom. He pressed the decompress button and air began to be pumped out of the airlock.

As soon as Ding heard the pumps, she banged on the glass with increased ferocity and desperation. Within twenty seconds she was gasping for air and had given up her attempts to break down the door. Several seconds later, the general watched in satisfaction as Ding lost consciousness. Her body went limp as the air pressure in the airlock dropped to less than ten percent. Zhang opened the outer airlock door and the momentum of the remaining escaping air carried Commander Ding's body slowly out into the freezing blackness of space. Once the body had drifted clear of the ship, the general closed the outer door and returned to the briefing room where everyone looked at him in expectant silence.

"Comrades," he said. "I think that sends a message to you and the rest of the crew. Thank you all for your ongoing support and understanding. I have chosen you to complete this important mission with me. It demands absolute loyalty. If anyone feels that they cannot give me that, they are free to join the commander."

There was a unanimous grunt of approval, although Zhang spotted fear in two of the crew. "I promise you that we will all return home as heroes. We are claiming Mars as our own and that mission starts today. Colonel Liu, you will remain here while I cross to *Taipei* with Major Huang Chen. I want comms locked down. No communication with

Earth is to take place without coming through me first. Any personal messages to loved ones cannot discuss what we are doing."

"Do you want me to contact Beijing?" Liu asked.

"No," replied the general. "The news of Commander Ding's unfortunate demise is best coming from me. There are likely to be some searching questions on the circumstances surrounding her death."

"Of course, general. The shuttlecraft is ready and at your disposal as soon as wish to leave."

"Excellent. I will leave in fifteen minutes, as soon as I have contacted Beijing. Major Huang, I expect you to be on board and ready to depart."

Huang nodded with some trepidation. She'd never spent time alone with the general and was fearful of making any errors.

Chapter 17

"Your girlfriend's been keeping secrets," Georgia snapped angrily when she finally found Jackson inside the cave complex constructing one of his prospecting drones. He was kneeling on the ground with his back to her, attaching four-foot-long rotor blades to one of the electric motors.

He paused immediately, noting the tone in her voice. "If it's that she has the hots for Captain Bailey then that's no secret, sis. I already told you. The whole crew knows. Except for the captain himself."

"No, it's nothing to do with that. This is serious. She and Molloy are here to turn Mars into a weapons testing ground. *Yorktown* was loaded with a new developmental particle beam weapon. Did you know anything about this?"

Jackson put down his tools and stood up. "Calm down, Georgia. Of course I didn't know. Why would I? I assume Bailey knows."

Georgia took a deep breath. "Yes, I had it out with him last night. That's how I found out. The program has been approved by the White House so there's nothing I can do about it."

"No wonder you're pissed. I can't believe they didn't inform you after what you've achieved here. Surely there must be something you can do. It's not like you to give up so easy."

"I could disrupt the testing. But our other friends on the planet are doing exactly the same thing. If I prevent Professor Duncan from completing her research, then I'm allowing other countries to get an advantage over us."

Captain Bailey's voice suddenly boomed from the darkness, less than ten yards away. "That wouldn't be a wise move, Georgia. But then neither is sharing classified information with your brother!"

"Oh fuck!" muttered Georgia. "Sir, you really shouldn't creep up on people like that."

"I followed you out. And it's a good thing that I did. Both of you to my quarters now. We need an urgent discussion, in private."

***

Standing stiffly in Bailey's quarters, Georgia was still fighting hard to control her feelings of anger and embarrassment at being caught out so easily. Keeping her emotions in check was a big problem for her at the moment. She immediately regretted speaking to Jackson. Now, he was standing next to her and in trouble through no fault of his own. In front of her, Captain Bailey was pacing up and down in silence, his hands clasped in front of him. It was making her uncomfortable.

"Sir, there's no reason for Jackson to be here," she pleaded. "He's done nothing wrong. I'm sure we can sort this out between us."

Bailey paused briefly, looked at her, and then continued his pacing.

Finally, he stopped and said. "You've put me in a very difficult situation. It's one thing to harangue Professor Duncan when she is following my orders. Sharing classified details of our mission with your brother is entirely different. It can easily put you both in jail for a very long time."

Georgia looked across at her brother who was now very pale and staring into the distance. She knew he wasn't enjoying any of this. He was a free spirit and not used to following orders. While she felt sorry for him, there was a matter of principle she had to deal with. "What did you expect when you told me about the weapons program? You turn up on my doorstep and want to turn my home into a firing range with no notice. It's a distinct lack of respect and trust."

"Trust works both ways!" Bailey shouted before taking a deep breath to calm himself. "I trusted you with the information I shared last night. I trusted that you could see I was sharing information when I had no authority to do so. I trusted that we could work together, with you as my deputy."

"Are you looking for trust or obedience?" Georgia replied, with no intention of backing down. "I can prove that I'm trustworthy. You've seen my record. But if you want a second in command that won't stand up to you or question some of your decisions, then you've picked the wrong person."

"Fuck it, Georgia. Take ownership for your mistake."

"I think she is taking ownership," interrupted Jackson. "But she doesn't think she's made a mistake. And neither do I."

Georgia couldn't help but smile, even as Bailey glared at both of them. She realized there was very little the captain could do to punish either of them without incriminating himself. The situation was awkward, to say the least.

After some further pacing, Bailey stopped in front of Jackson and said, "You're dismissed. Return to your work and say nothing about the weapon to anyone." Jackson looked questioningly at Georgia who directed him to leave while the going was good.

Bailey slumped into his chair and rubbed his eyes. "What am I to do with you though? Should I select someone else in your place?"

Georgia tried to make light of the situation. "You know what they say. Keep your friends close but your enemies closer."

"I don't want us to be enemies. You have so much experience to offer. Why are you getting so hung up on Professor Duncan's research?"

Georgia took a seat opposite Bailey, feeling calmer now that Jackson was no longer in the room. "You say that they have created the weapon to defend us against alien invasion. I don't buy that for a moment. Even if I did, the experience I had with the Sentinels was peaceful. They and the other alien species hold no more threat to us now than they did before we knew of their existence. The reaction of the president and other world leaders is irrational. The real reason for the weapons is far more subtle. It's to demonstrate which country has the biggest balls. Weapons testing on Mars is a sham. Each country wants to maintain its own national interests on this planet. I'm not convinced testing is required. I'd bet ten bucks that testing was completed months ago, and the weapon is fully operational."

The expression on Bailey's face was enough to confirm Georgia's suspicions.

"So, I'm right!" she exclaimed. "And you have the nerve to lecture me about trust when all the time you were lying to me."

Bailey looked defeated. "What did you really expect Georgia? The American government and multinational conglomerates have spent vast sums into this venture. Taxpayers and investors are expecting to see the returns that they were promised. The slightest hint of uncertainty and the financial support will come crashing down. Didn't you think they'd want to protect their investments?"

"Not by creating super weapons at great expense. There has to be a better way."

"Fear was the easiest way to access the trillions of dollars required to recruit and motivate the keenest minds and for development to be pushed through. To be fair, many of the scientists involved are convinced that the particle beam can deflect asteroids from destroying Earth."

"I'm still not convinced," said Georgia. "I want to speak with General Stockton."

"Are you sure? You won't get a different answer from him. He's been fully behind the weapon's development for eighteen months."

"The news just keeps getting better!" said Georgia, bitterly. "I need you both to reassure me that you're not holding anything else from me. You don't know how devastated at being kept out of the loop for so long."

***

As the quantum communications system still needed to be installed at the base, Georgia found herself one hour later on *Lexington*'s flight deck with Captain Bailey watching a recording General Stockton had made ten minutes earlier. His video was in direct response to an en-

crypted message from Georgia, with an introduction from Mac to explain the context.

The aging general appeared to be alone in his office back at Houston and was looking sharp in his dress uniform. Georgia supposed there
must be a formal event occurring. He looked troubled as he stared into
the camera. "Thank you for your message," he began. "I've been expecting it for some time although maybe not this soon. Georgia, I'm sorry
we could not brief you before *Lexington* arrived at Alpha Base. I'm sure
Mac has explained the situation to the best of his abilities and the need
for absolute discretion. I can totally understand your anger and disappointment at being kept in the dark for all this time. I take full responsibility for that decision and I remain convinced that I took the right
course of action in pursuit of the national interest.

"I knew you would object to the presence of the weapon. That is
not why you weren't told. There are more important decisions to be
made than considering your sensibilities. And while I am happy to have
ongoing frank and open discussions with you on this matter, you will
not dissuade me to mothball the particle beam program. The weapon
will be a key tool in the future defense of our nation on Earth and
America's assets on Mars and the Moon.

"Will we use the weapon against a hostile alien threat? I simply do
not know. I would tend to agree with your comment that it would be
suicidal to attack a more advanced civilization. If they are still observing us, then they must be aware of what we have created and are capable
of effecting suitable countermeasures.

"I sincerely hope that, like the huge arsenal of nuclear missiles we've
had at our disposal for the past sixty years, we never need to use this
weapon in anger. But the world is becoming a crazy place. With the
side effects of global warming increasing rapidly, oil reserves running
out and millions of people displaced by local conflicts, governments are
straining to deal with public outcry and civil unrest. I've seen nothing
like it, and I don't know what the future holds. So, in that atmosphere

of uncertainty, I ask you to trust me that we're doing the right thing. You don't have to like it, but I ask you to accept the situation. Stockton out."

Georgia stayed sitting in her chair looking at the screen. With the definitive response from the general, she found herself with nowhere to go. But at least she understood the truth. Any testing of the particle beam was to make it operational. Which meant that it was likely to stay in place for the foreseeable future. "Mac, am I to understand that the particle beam has already been deployed on Earth?"

"I never told you this, but several classified installations are being constructed across North America. Their sole purpose will be to shoot down any incoming missiles. There are also plans for two orbital platforms and installation on three of our aircraft carriers although, as Paige advised you, we are some way from an effective and accurate targeting system. Of course, those volumes will change if we discover the number of weapons being deployed by the Russians and Chinese. Theoretical modeling has shown that the weapon will be more effective on Mars and in space. That's because there's no real atmosphere to speak of that can degrade the beam."

"Wow, we really do mean business! There was I thinking that we were starting a new arms race when in reality that race began some time ago. What is the real reason for the weapon you brought with you?"

"Its primary purpose is a defense against unknown forces. We don't know what's going to happen on Earth. We do need to be prepared for the unexpected though. As the general said, we have some major investment here and we don't want to give them up easily if the balance of power changes back home."

"I hope you're right," said Georgia. "Knowing that there are weapons here makes me nervous. It means we're now a target."

Bailey stood up to make his way down to the cargo bay, and back down to their speeders on the surface. "We're a target anyway. The particle beam, once operational, will give us some teeth."

Georgia followed him down. "Am I still your second in command? I understand if you want someone else."

"I'm prepared to give you another chance if you'll do the same with me. We're both being influenced by politics outside of our control. If you still want to make a change, I suggest you'll have more success from the inside than as an outsider."

Georgia appreciated that Mac had a point. She'd lose any influence she may have if she was cast to the side. "Okay, Mac. But no more surprises."

Chapter 18

Even though *Taipei* was less than two thousand yards from *Shandong*, it took almost thirty minutes for Major Huang to pilot the shuttle between the two vehicles. General Zhang noted that she was far more cautious than she needed to be, but that was understandable. The approach to *Taipei's* docking port was a delicate operation and the many hours in the flight simulator in Beijing was not the same as flying the shuttle in orbit. There were no second chances out here.

Once securely docked, Huang was able to monitor the environmental systems on *Taipei*. The systems had been powered down for the trip to Mars in order to save power. Although Colonel Liu had remotely activated life support as soon as they had entered orbit, the interior temperature had still not reached a comfortable level. "I'm sorry general, but we'll have to enter in our pressure suits and helmets. It will be several hours before the ship is habitable once again."

Zhang was annoyed by the inconvenience but wasn't prepared to wait another few hours. Huang helped the general climb into his pressure suit before passing through the airlock into *Taipei*. The interior was basic and lit with harsh red LED lights, which his eyes quickly became accustomed to. The corridor leading to the control center was a tight in his spacesuit, but he was able to pull himself along a ladder without too much difficulty.

The control room itself held three banks of computer equipment and screens, designed so that the weapon could be operated by two people. The main screen incorporated the targeting scanner which, at the moment was blank. A third seat was for a pilot in the event that the flight computer could not be relied of.

Zhang lowered himself into his seat, strapped himself in and keyed in the command code to power up the ship. Immediately, various colored lights flashed across the banks of equipment and the screens flickered into life. Zhang held his breath, waiting for warning lights to appear. The next few minutes would let him know if the ship was fully operational.

Major Huang had also strapped herself into her seat and was monitoring the startup sequence, also waiting for any discrepancies to appear. After five minutes, both of them were satisfied to see that no red warning lights had appeared on the screens. "All systems are working, general. The only minor issue is that the batteries have been drained during the journey and currently are at sixty-eight percent of full capacity."

"That is not enough to fire the weapon," replied Zhang. "How long will it take to charge the batteries?"

"The solar panels have been deployed but the environmental systems have been drawing more power in order to get the ship back to temperature. I would estimate another ten hours until the batteries have recharged to ninety percent. That will be enough power to fire the weapon two or three times depending on the duration and the beam intensity."

The continuing delays were testing Zhang's fragile patience, but on this occasion, he knew there was nothing he could do but wait. The technical issues were way beyond his level of expertise. "Okay, major, I am satisfied that there are no obvious problems. Do whatever you can to restore battery storage. Is there anything else we need to do here?"

"I don't believe so, general. Other than the batteries, the ship is in perfect health."

"Then return me to *Shandong* so that we may determine the next steps."

***

Back in *Shandong*'s briefing room, his senior and most loyal officers surrounded General Zhang. Colonel Liu was the first to speak. "Sir, I have received a communication from Beijing. They have received your message and pass on their condolences for the commander's sad loss. They would, however, appreciate a more detailed report from you explaining the circumstances surrounding Commander Ding's death. It sounds as if they intend to carry out a full inquiry."

"I expected nothing less. The sudden death of any senior officer has to be fully explained. The matter is not important at the moment, and I will deal with it when the time is right. I am more interested to hear how the crew have taken the news."

"There has been the odd voice of dissent, general," replied Liu. "The situation has come as a sudden shock, but they understand the situation they are in. We have reassured them that you will take care of them and there is no necessity for any further... examples to be made."

Zhang addressed the room. "Thank you all for your efficient execution of this first stage of our plan. Now we can move on to the next phase. The particle beam weapon has survived the trip from Earth and the batteries are currently being charged to full capacity. My intent is to test it tomorrow morning. All that is left is to agree on which target to hit first."

Colonel Liu switched on the main computer screen and brought up a graphical representation of the Martian surface with the Russian and American bases highlighted. Using the navigation computer, Liu added an overlay of *Shandong*'s orbits around Mars for the following twenty-four hours. "You will see, general, that we pass very close to the Russian base on this orbit here." Liu pointed to a green line circling the planet. "We will have thirty-eight seconds when the base will be in range of *Taipei*. We will have similar opportunities on the subsequent two orbits but then we would have to wait a further seventeen hours until our we pass over the base again."

"I understand," replied a frustrated Zhang, although he was confused by the myriad numbers and symbols in front of him. Orbital mechanics was not one of his strengths, unlike knowing when to strike his enemy at the optimum moment. "What about the Americans? Can we take them by surprise?"

Liu nodded his head. "That is why I suggested this particular orbit. It will take us five degrees north of Alpha Base fifteen minutes after we have obliterated the Russians. We will have a direct line of sight, allowing us maybe ten seconds in which to fire a particle burst from a low angle. From that range, I cannot guarantee the accuracy of our targeting computers, and at best we could only attack one location. Their ships are spread wide and the base is protected by the cliff face."

"That is most unfortunate. When will we have a better opportunity?"

"Eight orbits later we will be in the correct inclination to take three or four clear shots."

"That's no good," replied Zhang, shaking his head. "By then, the Americans will know about our attack on Derzost and be prepared for us. I want a preemptive strike. What is the status of the American weapon?"

"The latest satellite imagery reveals that the Americans are in a hurry. They've already unloaded equipment from their ship. We can only surmise that they are preparing to test their weapon very soon, but we do not know when."

Zhang frowned. If the Americans had time to prepare, they could establish their own weapon and potentially take out *Taipei* or *Shandong* and he would have lost his advantage. "Suggestions anyone?"

Major Huang said, "may I remind the general that the attack on Derzost will deplete the batteries. We may not have enough power to fire the particle beam again within fifteen minutes."

Liu nodded, "that is true, sir. We may have no choice but to wait."

"Stop telling me what I can't do," shouted Zhang, causing everyone in the room to cringe. "Give me a solution."

One of the junior officers at the back of the room spoke up. "General, we only need to disable the Russian base on the first pass. If we target one location, their control center for instance, we could conserve enough power for an attack on the American weapon. With both bases disabled, we can complete the attacks on later orbits at our leisure."

Zhang searched his memory for the officer's name, cursing inwardly that he was finding it more difficult as he got older. "Thank you, Colonel Xi. That is the tactical thinking I expect from you all. You're right. As long as we can cripple both bases, then we are well on our way to owning this planet. Colonel Liu, what do you think?"

Colonel Liu was irked that the suggestion had not come from him. "I will need to run some calculations, general. But I believe it will be feasible. Of course, we still don't know the effect our particle beam will have at full power. It has never been fired in anger from outer space. There are lots of unknowns at this time."

"I have more confidence in our scientists than you," replied Zhang. "It will work as designed. Once we have demonstrated its capabilities, I have no doubt it will go into mass construction on Earth, allowing us to retake the high ground there as well. It will be the greatest weapon in our armory."

"One more question, sir," said Huang. "What about our scientists on Derzost? Shouldn't we warn them to leave before we carry out our attack?"

Zhang glared as if a child had asked him a simple question. "Major, do you want to give our enemy advance warning? Maybe I should contact Derzost's commander now and tell him our plan! No, unfortunately the two scientists will be innocent casualties of war. Their names and their sacrifice will be remembered though. And we will honor their deaths by successfully completing our mission and eradicating all other nations from Mars. Is that clear?"

"Perfectly, general," replied a chastened Major Huang, conscious that everyone was staring at her.

"Good! In that case, everyone is dismissed. Liu, I want your calculations in the next hour. I respect your tactical knowledge so tell me where to strike and how many particle bursts will be required for both targets."

The room emptied, leaving Zhang to stare at the projection of Mars on the computer screen. With the lull in activities, he felt drained and fatigued as his adrenaline levels subsided. He'd felt this before when preparing for major battles. His body was saving its energy for the big offensive. He knew from experience that, when the time was right, he'd be fully alert and capable of making the decisive action. Until then, it was a waiting game.

Chapter 19

Professor Anna Kozlovsky was unpacking a small crate in the main science lab when Redmayne entered. He watched her for several moments, noticing, now that she was wearing jeans and a crew neck shirt, how slim she was. She was moving slowly and deliberately as she carefully picked up items from the crate.

"Can I help you with that?" he asked. "I know it takes a few days to adjust to the effects of gravity. You need to be cautious while your central nervous system and muscles adapt. Don't lift anything too heavy."

She was about to decline his offer but then changed her mind. What was the point in struggling? "As you're here you may as well make yourself useful. Can you lift those boxes onto the counter? And be careful, they contain very delicate instruments."

As Redmayne stepped forward to oblige, Kozlovsky moved away, keeping a safe distance between the two of them before sitting wearily on a stool. He wasn't surprised by her action as he was sure that some of the crew would have warned her to stay away from him. He wondered how different she may have been if she was unaware of the terrible things he'd done. "Alex said you were ready to see me. Is that to brief me on the experiments I'll be working on?"

Her eyebrows furrowed. "I knew this was a mistake. Your ego precedes you. Let me make myself clear one more time. You will be working for me and helping me gather the results of the experiments. If you find that difficult to accept, then I suggest you speak with Commander Koenig who no doubt has far more interesting tasks for you to undertake."

Redmayne was weary of the menial jobs that had been given to him and the way he'd been treated over the last twelve months. The prospect of working in the science lab again was a welcome relief. Hopefully, it was the first step in cementing his usefulness to the Russians. "There's no need to do that, Anna," he replied. "I am more than happy to assist you in any way. And to learn from you, of course."

"Let's stick to Professor Kozlovsky, Mister Redmayne. Informality and familiarity are not productive to establishing strong working relationships."

"In that case, please call me Doctor Redmayne, Professor."

There was an awkward silence as Anna weighed up whether Redmayne was worth the effort. In the end she asked, "Has anyone spoken to you about the experiments I'll be conducting?"

"You've got to be joking! No one tells me anything. I'm sorry to admit I don't even know what you specialize in."

Anna nodded. "That's probably a good thing as the work is highly confidential. I've been leading a skilled group of scientists on a classified project to develop a particle beam device, primarily as a form of defense in response to the knowledge that we are not alone in the Universe. President Usimov and his generals were rightfully fearful that the Russian Federation was unable to defend itself effectively against an alien attack. The work we will be performing here is the culmination of my two years' extensive research."

The information was not what Redmayne had been expecting. He said, "I'm not an expert on the subject but my understanding is that there is an inherent issue with particle beams as they tend to diverge due to mutual repulsion. That makes them ineffectual by the time they reach the intended target. What have you done to remedy that flaw?"

"I'm shocked by your knowledge," she replied. "You are correct that there is a problem with charged particle beams. However, we've been able to create a neutral-particle-beam weapon that first ionizes atoms before accelerating the particles through a cyclotron. The limited proof-of-concept tests we've been able to perform on Earth have been successful, but we need to perform them on a larger scale."

"Very impressive. I assume you've brought the weapon to Mars to avoid any publicity, on the basis that direct energy weapon have been outlawed. You didn't think to share your work with other countries in order to save the whole of humanity, not just the Russian Federation."

"We needed to carry out the tests across large distances and in near vacuum. Mars seemed a logical choice. We can point the weapon at one of the moons to determine its effectiveness. And as for collaborating with other nations, you may like to know that both the Americans and the Chinese have brought their own versions of a particle beam weapon to test. Ours is not the first to arrive on Mars."

"Great! The three superpowers have entered into a new arms race. On the pretense that it's to save the Earth. In reality, it's just an excuse for the respective army generals to have new more powerful and highly efficient ways of killing innocent citizens."

"I hear you know about killing innocent people. You have at least three murders to your name."

Redmayne blanched but was unable to defend himself. "Yes, there were unfortunate consequences to my actions, and I regret what occurred. It doesn't mean I condone the creation of new weapons. Have you seriously thought through the consequences of your actions? They could be more catastrophic than the deaths of three people."

"That is not for you to question, Redmayne. You're here to assist me in completing the testing and proving that the technology will work in the environment. But I will not allow the power of the Russian Federation to be usurped by foreign powers. Any concerns you have should be directed at them."

"I'm simply sharing my opinion with you. I know this work has been your focus for many years and I'm sure your research to date has been impeccable. I just question the practical uses that the weapon is likely to be put to and if your conscience is prepared for it."

Anna hesitated. But before she could respond, Captain Stepanov entered the room, and she stood sharply to attention. "Relax Professor," he said. "Is everything okay in here? I heard raised voices."

"I was briefing Redmayne on the research he'll be helping me with. He appears to have some moral reservations."

"Really?" replied Stepanov. "Does that make him an unsuitable assistant for you?

Anna stared across at Redmayne, "I'm not sure."

Redmayne felt he was being set up. "I did not realize I was not able to question the research. I've often found it useful to have someone to bounce ideas off. Someone who doesn't necessarily hold my views. After all, two intelligent brains are better than one. However, if you simply want a silent but able assistant, then I will do that to the best of my abilities."

Stepanov looked doubtful. "I don't like you or why you're here. In fact, I think everyone on this base has that same opinion of you. I'm sure you know that if you are as intelligent as you claim to be. There would be no tears shed if, one day, you disappeared."

"Thank you for clarifying that, Captain Stepanov. I am very aware of my standing in the base. Which is why I will be a very obedient and effective assistant for Professor Kozlovsky."

"That is much better." Stepanov turned to face the Professor. "If you have any further concerns with this man, please let me know immediately. I will gladly and swiftly rectify the situation personally." After glaring at Redmayne again for one final time, he walked to the doorway and added, "By the way, Professor. Commander Koenig is holding a reception for all the new arrivals in one hour."

Once Stepanov had left, Redmayne muttered, "I guess my invitation must be lost in the post."

Anna heard him and laughed. It was the first time he'd seen her smile, and it was glorious. "I'll say one thing about you, Redmayne. You're the most resilient person I've known. You are going to be a very challenging man to work with. But maybe you can bring some valuable insight to the research. Remember who's in change and you may just get to see the completion of the work. As for what happens to the technology once proved, well that's way above my pay grade. I think we're done here for the day. I need a rest before the reception."

"Okay. When do we start?"

"Tomorrow. Your first task is to take the power meter in that box and attach it to the transducer located at the solar farm. We need to establish if sufficient electricity is being generated to power the cyclotron on an ongoing basis. I have a bad feeling that we're going to have to extend the solar farm before we can carry out meaningful testing. The commander won't thank us if the power cuts out every time we fire up the weapon. And while you're on the surface, can you retrieve a canister that's attached to the side of *Tolstoy*? You can't miss it as it has my initials on the lid." She stood up and slowly left the room.

Redmayne was filled with conflicted emotions as he watched her leave. On the one hand, he'd been given another chance to perform important research, while on the other he was helping to create a powerful weapon that could lead to a war. Although he had once wanted the Russians to dominate the West, he had come to realize that each side was as evil and corrupt as the other. It was a surprise that Georgia Pyke would allow the Americans to carry out similar research. She was such an idealist and was the last person he expected to condone weapons development on Mars, especially against her beloved alien friends. He wondered how much she actually knew.

Chapter 20

Georgia had decided an early morning visit to the biodome might sooth her frustrations. The natural smells from the plants and vegetables, together with the gurgling of the water filters, was the closest to the feeling of being back on Earth, especially if she closed her eyes and ran her fingers through the leaves. It was rare that she felt the need to visit the biodome, but it always improved her mood and provided clarity of thought.

This morning, it seemed that Megan had a similar idea as she entered the biodome less than five minutes after Georgia.

"Are you here to get your head straight as well?" asked Megan.

Georgia nodded. "You could say that I have a few issues on my mind. I guess *Lexington*'s arrival is harder to adjust to than I expected. There are too many surprises and changes for my liking."

"How are you finding the new arrivals? They appear to have made themselves at home very quickly." There was something about the way Megan phrased her question that made Georgia suspect the doctor wasn't overly impressed. Perhaps that was why she was also in the biodome that morning. But dealing with Megan's problems could be a welcome distraction from her own dissatisfaction.

"Too early to tell. I've only met a few of them really. The captain is great, obviously. I'm less enamored with some of the military aspects of their mission but I can't go into it now." She realized she needed to be more discrete and was still likely to rant about the particle beam weapon if she started on the subject. Instead, she pushed the conversation back towards her friend. "How are you and Doctor Coleman getting on? Is he growing on you yet?"

Megan's scowl said more than words ever could. "I may defect to the Russians if he keeps on. The man has no bedside manner whatsoever."

"Have you considered that he didn't expect to find you here? When he signed on to the program, his role was going to be chief physician for the base. Then you go and change your plans and suddenly he's having to share that role with someone with two years' experience of life on Mars. I think he's entitled to be slightly pissed off."

"I can't believe you're defending him. I'm supposed to be your best friend. I've always had your back," said Megan.

"I'm not defending Doctor Coleman. I agree he's been totally unbearable, and I sympathize with you. All I'm asking is that you see the matter from his perspective. If you understand what his real beef is, you may be able to come up with an amicable truce. It could be he's intimidated by you and your reputation."

"You're right," agreed Megan, with a devious smile. "I have set a very high bar in my time here. Just look at the medical research I've completed as well as the papers I've had published. You can't really blame Doctor Coleman for feeling inadequate."

***

After breakfast, Georgia wandered up to the control room where Captain Bailey was standing in her usual spot, staring out of the large viewing window. "I've been watching the sunrise," he said, turning to her. "The same sun but a different planet. It's hard to get my head around. I don't even know how long I've been standing here watching the sun's rays lighting up more and more of the cliff face before it lit up the plain. Shadows creeping from unseen boulders and the occasional dust devil in the distance. It's a new world and I think I'm beginning to see what you do."

Georgia shrugged nonchalantly. "I didn't think it would take you long to see what I want to defend here. With a lot of hard work, we could make this world habitable. It will take generations, but anything is possible with a little imagination and a lot of ambition."

"I don't doubt it for one moment, Georgia. Not if you have any-thing to do with it. But down to business. I'm going out to *Yorktown* with Professor Duncan and Lieutenant Molloy. I want to oversee the assembly of the particle beam weapon. And I want to update them on your position."

"My position hasn't really changed. I still object to the weapon be-ing here. The same goes for the Russians and Chinese. But I am willing to be practical and support you as best I can, although I have no inter-est in seeing the weapon actually fired."

Bailey nodded, appreciatively. "Thank you for being so understand-ing. I do share some of your reservations. We will find a way of making this work over the next few weeks and months. What are your plans for today?"

"Aquaponics this morning. I'm introducing your two horticultur-ists to the progress started by the Kings. Mancuso is beside himself that he no longer has to care for the plants. He doesn't have the greenest fin-gers, but he didn't kill any of the crops, so he can't be that bad."

"Maybe I'll pay a visit there later today. I'd really like to see lettuces being grown on Mars."

"We have so much more than that," Georgia said smugly. "There are still lessons to be learned but we are beginning to grow enough to have regular fresh greens. I think you'll be impressed by the sights and the smell. Let me know when you're free and I'll give you a personal tour."

Bailey smiled warmly. "I'll definitely take you up on that offer."

***

Eighteen hundred miles northwest of Alpha Base, Redmayne began suiting up for his excursion to the solar farm. Romansky saw him by the airlock as he tested the seals on his boots and gloves. "Hey, Predatel, you know you shouldn't really go out alone. We may decide not to let you back in again." Romansky laughed out loud at his own joke while Redmayne did his best to ignore him.

It was clear to Redmayne that Romansky was looking to wind him up. The gruff engineer moved closer, his breath stinking of stale vodka and fermenting cabbage. Had his life really come to this, Redmayne wondered. "Have they have sent you to run more errands for the sexy professor? I saw her disappear into the captain's quarters late last night so don't think you can charm your way around her."

Redmayne felt a flash of anger and clenched his fists. But seeing that Romansky was ready for a fight, he relaxed. "That is none of my business, Romansky. And it shouldn't be any of yours. I'm helping Professor Kozovsky carry out important research. What are you doing, other than getting very drink?"

"Pray that I'm not here when you return, or you may find the airlock won't work. I'll see that you never return to Earth alive."

Redmayne stood up and entered the inner airlock door. He was concerned that in his current drunken state, Romansky was capable of anything. All he could hope for was that the big Russian slept it off. Perhaps another talk with Alex later would help.

Checking that he had the professor's equipment, he closed the airlock door, sealed the visor on his helmet and depressurized the compartment before opening the outer door and stepping outside. The low sun shone directly into his face, turning the fine scratches on his Plexiglas visor into a complex spider's web pattern that obstructed his vision. Cursing that he'd forgotten to wear his sunglasses, he stepped carefully across the open terrain toward the solar farm. He was in no hurry this morning. Most of the crew were sleeping off vodka induced hangovers, and it sounded as if Anna was otherwise occupied.

***

Near the base of *Yorktown*, assembly of the particle beam weapon was almost complete thanks to Molloy's skills and technical expertise. Captain Bailey could only be fascinated by the speed and dexterity with which he was fitting the components together. The captain was taking a break with Paige, in the shadow of one of *Yorktown*'s landing fins in order to keep his suit cool.

"Charlie's just a beast at this sort of thing," he said to Paige. "I was impressed during training but never expected him to be this quick on Mars."

Paige was less enthusiastic. "He's been a caged animal for the past three months. What did you expect? He has to burn up that nervous energy somehow."

"I can still hear you both," added Molloy. "During my time in the army we trained often and hard for repetitive activities such as this. We had to learn to dismantle and rebuild our rifles in the dark after days of little sleep and in stressful conditions. The secret was to memorize the sequence and block out all extraneous stimuli. It was tough, but the training is designed to save lives. This task is not much different. It would, however, be great if I could have your assistance on some of the larger items. You can't expect me to align them on my own and achieve the precision required."

"Okay, we get the hint," replied Bailey. "How much longer do you think we need?"

"Two hours max," replied Molloy.

"That works out fine," said Paige. "The construction robot should have run the power cable as far as the reactor by then. We just need someone to plug it in at that end and we'll be ready to go."

"I'll radio Alpha Base from the MEV and have Rashid Qadir on standby," said Captain Bailey.

"That can wait twenty minutes, sir," said Molloy. "I need you to pass me the first of the electron emitter electrodes from that box over there. And there's seven more where that came from. Please be gentle with them; they're highly sensitive components."

"You told me the same thing when I was unpacking the particle accelerator," complained Bailey.

"I know. The electrodes are even more sensitive. And we have only two spares."

"By the way," added Bailey, as he remembered his earlier conversation. "Georgia Pyke is beginning to accept the presence of this weapon. She had a long heart to heart with myself and General Stockton and I think she may be softening her approach."

Paige looked up from where she was standing. "I find that hard to believe after she gave me such a hard time yesterday. She's a tree hugger who would be happy if mankind never progressed beyond bows and arrows."

"You need to see it from her point of view as well. She'd only just found out what we're doing here and that she'd been deceived. I don't know if I would have reacted any differently in her position."

"Maybe not," conceded Paige. "But the woman is paranoid. I think she's been on Mars too long. She was more interested in the consequences of the base being attacked by a particle beam weapon. Her first thought was what happens if the base is attacked by a particle beam fired from space."

Molloy laughed. "She's seen too many science fiction movies. I hope you explained why that was impossible."

"Of course. Maybe my expert analysis was what helped convert her to our side."

"I wouldn't say she's a convert just yet," cautioned Bailey. "But she's on the way. Just give her some time."

Chapter 21

General Zhang was strapped tightly in his seat on *Taipei* and could feel the adrenaline flowing through him. Now was the time for battle. It had been far too long since he'd had this feeling of exhilaration. He felt young and vibrant, even invincible. Engaging the enemy was the second best natural high he could imagine, bettered only by the glory of victory.

This precise moment had been years in the making. Although the detailed plans had altered dramatically over the years as technology advanced, he knew the performance and outcome would remain as intended. China would reassert its dominance and demonstrate its power to the rest of the world.

Alongside Zhang, Colonel Liu was busy readying the weapon for its first real use in anger. Major Huang sat in the pilot's seat, checking the ship's systems for any faults or potential issues. As he watched his crew calmly performing their tasks, Zhang took comfort that there was no sense of urgency or drama from either of them. There would be no mistakes.

Below them, Mars was in darkness. The main view screen was unable to discern any features. That would change soon enough though with sunrise. Although unnecessary for their advanced targeting system, Derzost would be clearly lit by the sun when the attack was ready to begin.

"How long until we are over the target?" he asked Huang.

"We will be in range in twenty-eight minutes, general. I am about to move *Taipei* a safe distance from the rest of the convoy and orient the ship, so the particle beam is directed at the planet."

"Good work. How are the power levels?"

Colonel Liu briefly glanced at the computer display to the right of him. "The batteries are almost fully charged. They will be at a minimum ninety-nine percent capacity by the time we overfly the Russians. That will allow us to fire the beam at full power for thirty seconds. More than enough time to breach their shielding."

"Use only what you have to in order to incapacitate their base," reminded the general. "I want to be able to hit the Americans with as much force as we can. We can't afford them time to set up their own weapon."

"We will monitor the impact of the beam but remember that it has never been fully tested. The attack on Derzost will be the first time we get to understand what we are capable of."

Zhang ignored the warning and stared at Liu. "Do what you must but ensure we immobilize the American weapon."

***

Professor Anna Kozovsky stirred slowly as she awoke with a pounding headache. As she lay in the near darkness trying to get her bearings in the strange environment, she was appalled to hear someone breathing in the bed next to her. She reached out a hand and felt the warm, hard, muscular body of a man. She gasped as the hazy memories of the previous night gradually formed in her mind. Captain Stepanov! What had she been thinking?

She slowly rolled herself out of the bunk, careful not to make a noise or disturb the still sleeping Stepanov. She was dismayed to see clothes strewn across the room. It must have been some night, she thought although she couldn't really remember much of it. She was confident she hadn't drunk that much. As she put her clothes back on, she hoped that no one had seen her with the captain. The last thing she needed was a reputation for being easy or people gossiping about her behind her back. She couldn't think of a worse possible start to her stay at Derzost.

She had almost made it to the door when Stepanov startled her. "Leaving without saying goodbye, Anna?" he said from his bed. "We had a good time last night. I hope you don't feel ashamed that you gave in to temptation."

"Grigory, I can't remember much about last night to be ashamed of. But this shouldn't have happened. It is not good for either of our reputations amongst the crew."

"I disagree. Any woman would be honored to spend a night with me. And the men will be envious that I have slept with the most beautiful woman on the planet. If anything, it will enhance both our reputations. This is a good thing, no?"

Anna couldn't believe what she'd just heard. Well she could. He was an army man after all. "I think we'll leave it there," she replied. "We clearly have a different perspective on the merits of sleeping with colleagues. I need to get back to my room and take some painkillers. I'd forgotten what vodka does to me."

Stepanov smiled at her embarrassment. He stood up, still naked, and came toward her. "One more kiss, for old times' sake?" he teased.

Anna looked momentarily horrified. "Thanks, but no." And without another word, she fumbled the door open and left as fast as she could.

Her own quarters were only three doors away and she thankfully made it without anyone spotting her. After quickly washing down two painkillers with a glass of water, she grabbed a towel and headed to the showers thinking that her day could only improve.

***

Redmayne was already at the solar farm, attempting to remove the access panel from the transducer. Although he had the correct tool, the accumulation of dust had caused the mechanism to seize. He doubted that anyone had opened the unit since it had been first installed. So far, he'd spent fifteen minutes fruitlessly trying different ways to open the panel. He appreciated he couldn't return to the base without successfully installing the monitor. It should be a simple task and was the first one set by Professor Kozovsky. He needed to demonstrate what he was capable of.

He removed a knife from his utility belt and slid it around the rim of the panel, hoping to find some leverage or at least clear any offending dust. When that failed, he tried once more with the locking mechanism. This time, he was rewarded with some movement as he applied pressure. He felt a bead of sweat run down the side of his face as he continued to exert more pressure until he eventually sensed the lock release. "About bloody time!" he shouted in relief as he lifted the panel out and placed it on the ground.

Peering inside the transducer, he could see the port he would connect the monitor unit too. Thankfully, this was a more straightforward task and two minutes later he was closing the panel back up again.

Redmayne stood, stretched his legs to get the circulation going again and did his best to brush the dust from his suit. Not for the first time he looked back at the low single-story domes that comprised the base. He was sure that the new habitation modules to be delivered in the next following weeks would improve living conditions, but it would still not be up to the standard he was used to. They'd be fine for the Russian miners he expected to arrive in a further two years, and he hoped he was long gone by then. The thought of sharing a confined space with burly Russians, with no sense of proprietary, made him shiver.

The two landing craft about a mile from where he was standing were still his best option of escape. He'd flown in *Kiev* several times to ferry supplies from the Russian ships in orbit. Although he was no pilot, he now understood how most of the semi-automated flight systems operated. The second ship that had just arrived, *Tolstoy*, was supposed to be more advanced with a fully autonomous system that would allow incapacitated crewmen to be returned to *Moskva* in the case of an extreme emergency. It was simply a matter of waiting for the right opportunity to present itself.

***

"Target acquisition in twenty seconds, general." Zhang could hear the controlled excitement in Major Huang's voice. The long-awaited anticipation of action would soon be replaced with the fulfillment of warfare.

On the main screen in front of them, Zhang could see the Martian landscape scrolling by. The early morning sun causing long dark shadows from rocky escarpments and craters. At the top of the screen, he could see the Russian base coming into range. The layout looked exactly as the satellite images he'd been studying although he could now spot a second landing craft that had not been there when the images were taken. The dust and rock that covered the base was an effective camouflage against the desert. However, the vast array of solar panels and the many tracks created by wheeled vehicles provided sufficient evidence of human presence.

"Aim for the control center, just below the main antenna," he instructed, pointing to the screen. He noted his hand was shaking slightly. Stay calm and focused, he reminded himself.

Colonel Liu called out, "batteries are now at one hundred percent. The particle accelerator has been cooled to minus one hundred and forty. All lights are green. The weapon is ready to be activated at your command, General Zhang."

Each of the crew held their breath as they watched the clock count down to zero. They understood that there would be no going back from what they were about to do. Their action would commit China and alter its destiny forever. But, as one, each of them was absolutely convinced they were doing the right thing.

Zhang made a final check that the targeting laser was pointed at the correct spot on the Russian base before assuredly ordering, "Now Colonel."

Colonel Liu pressed the red firing button in front of him. There was an immediate deafening hum as the power transferred to the particle beam weapon and the internal lights flickered and died. Zhang felt the air around him tingle and the whole ship buzz. On the main screen, it appeared as if nothing had changed. Derzost looked exactly the same and was intact, the main dome dominating the image.

The general was confused and angry. "What's happening? What has gone wrong with the weapon?"

"Nothing, sir. All systems remain nominal," replied Liu calmly. "It will take several seconds for the beam to penetrate the walls of the base. Please continue to watch the monitor"

Zhang peered closed at the screen. After several seconds, he thought he briefly saw some smoke rising from the target area but the next moment he was taken by surprise as the roof of the Russian base erupted in a massive explosion. He saw computers, chairs and even two people blown through the gaping hole and landing maybe fifty feet away.

"Particle beam shut down. Power reserves at eighty five percent," confirmed Major Huang.

"From initial observations, the Russian base has lost all of its internal atmosphere. There was too much escaping debris and gas just from their control room," said Liu. "We've heard reports from our scientists that the Russians are lazy and don't close their internal seals."

"If that is the case, they learned a hard lesson today," said Huang with a satisfied smile.

Zhang's initial doubts were appeased with the deadly efficiency of the weapon. It had far exceeded his expectations and taken less than fifteen seconds to severely disable and possibly destroy the Russian base. From the size of the blast, he doubted there would be any survivors from the attack and no evidence as to the immediate cause of the blast. Now to catch the Americans off guard as well. Then it would be time to consider a small victory celebration.

***

Redmayne stared in outright horror as equipment and bodies continued to fly into the air from the rupture in Derzost's dome and rain down next to the Russian base. It was like a ghoulish fountain. From this far away, he could accurately count the bodies, but he was sure he'd seen at least six. They must be dead as he'd not seen any wearing spacesuits.

He'd already seen enough bodies on Mars to last him a lifetime. He didn't want to see any more. He stayed where he was, watching as the escaping gas subsided and waiting for anything else to happen

Just before the explosion, he'd noticed a faint beam of purple light shining on the Russian base. Looking up he'd seen a brief flash of something metallic at the far end of the beam, traveling at high speed across the cloudless sky. But before his mind had been able to make sense of what he was looking at, his attention had been drawn to the sudden eruption of Derzost's roof as the internal atmosphere escaped, taking whatever was loose with it. The beam of light ceased as quickly as it began but Redmayne was more concerned with what he should do next. It was evident the base had been attacked, but by whom? He suddenly felt very exposed and vulnerable.

He looked around him for any more impacts from the attack. Both landing craft looked as if they had escaped any damage from the explosion. That was the only positive he could think of. He contemplated whether he should escape in one of the craft before the attackers returned or should he return to the base and search for survivors. After the way they had mistreated him, he felt that he owed them nothing. He hoped that Romansky, in particular, had not made it. Alex had saved his life after being left to die on the surface and was the only person who had shown him any consideration. He was the only one worth saving.

He calculated that, all things considered, he stood a better chance of survival if he could find anyone alive in what was left of Derzost. With a heavy heart he started to trudge back toward the base, glancing up often on the lookout for any more strange signs in the sky. He set his mind to why someone would carry out a pre-emptive strike on the Russian base. The obvious aggressor had to be either the Americans or Chinese, taking advantage of their own particle beam research. There was also the remote possibility the Sentinels or another alien species had attacked. Redmayne's money was on the Chinese as he knew their ships were still in orbit. The Americans could also have a ship orbiting the planet, but this type of attack wasn't their style. Was this the first step in a Chinese invasion of the base? He stopped in his tracks. Were the two Chinese scientists waiting for him?

He looked again at the carnage in front of him. It would have taken a brave or foolish person to have remained inside waiting for the attack to happen. If the Chinese had attacked the base in such a fashion, then they would have no qualms in sacrificing two of their own countrymen. He continued forward again, warily stepping around some of the remains of Derzost that now littered his path.

Having had some time to compose his thoughts, he began to realize that the sudden attack was possibly the opportunity he'd been looking for. He now had a perfectly valid excuse to return to *Moskva* and request a return to Earth. The Russians would be desperate to understand what had occurred. As the only witness, his testimony would be invaluable. And if he also managed to save anyone from the wreckage his redemption would be complete. All he had to do was survive long enough to make it back to one of the landing craft.

Chapter 22

Paige Duncan snapped the final set of connectors into place, confirmed by three green lights on the control console in front of her. It had taken several attempts, but the diagnostics check was showing that the system was ready to be powered up. Seeing that no one was paying her any attention, she punched the air with satisfaction. It had taken many years of research, working weekends and nights, to get to this moment. Having her pet project finally ready for testing on Mars made all that dedication and personal sacrifice worthwhile. She fully recognized, though, that there was still plenty of work ahead of her and Molloy.

"Charlie, I believe we have an operating particle beam ready to test. Thank you so much for all your commitment to the project. I'm sure we wouldn't be where we are without your focus and genius."

Molloy hopped across and gave her a high five. "Don't sell yourself short, Paige. It's your leadership that was the glue to our success. To be fair, I had my doubts we'd be testing so soon when the diagnostics failed the first few times. I was convinced we'd damaged some components two days ago."

"Congratulations to both of you," added Captain Bailey, who had been watching silently as they'd tried to troubleshoot the final issues. He could do no more than act as a spectator as they had made the minutest adjustments to the delicate equipment. "It's a fantastic effort for America. General Stockton will be immensely impressed when we report the good news to him later. What happens next?"

Paige walked up to him, keen to show what her new pet project could do. "The weapon is running on internal batteries at the moment. That's enough to power the console and sensors but that's all. As soon as Rashid connects us to the reactor, we'll have sufficient power to start the particle accelerator. With luck, we can commence some very low power tests this afternoon. That will enable us to perform calibration of the various components and shake out any unexpected anomalies.

Once those tests are complete, we'll gradually increase the energy of the particle beam until it's at full power."

"Rashid said he'll have us connected within thirty minutes," replied Bailey. "We may as well take a break in the MEV and wait for his call. I don't know about you youngsters, but my legs are ready to collapse."

Molloy said, "You go ahead. I want to check the electron emitters one more time. I've learned you can never take anything for granted."

Paige understood there was no point trying to dissuade him. She'd known Molloy long enough to accept his pedantic eye for detail. She, however, was grateful for Captain Bailey's suggestions after spending three hours in her spacesuit. She was looking forward to removing her helmet and having some refreshment. She raced to catch up with the captain who was already climbing up into the MEV's airlock.

***

Georgia found Mancuso in the control room, transferring data from his tablet to the master computer. "You'll be pleased to hear your caretaker duties in aquaponics is officially over. *Lexington*'s two horticulturists, Kelly and Dryden, have said you did an excellent job," she told him.

"At least the Kings have someone else to pester. I've enough to do, assisting with the unloading and storage of supplies. Don't get me wrong, Vicky Morris is exceptional at her job, but she's hampered by her injured foot."

"I know you'll give her all the help she needs. You like helping damsels in distress. You've helped me more times than I care to remember."

"That's because we're a family, Georgia. And families look out for one another." Mancuso paused for a moment, before asking. "I'm also concerned about you. What are you doing about the weapon over at *Yorktown*?"

Georgia frowned at the direct question. Mancuso never failed to surprise her but, other than Megan, he was the one she trusted to give her honest feedback and support. "I'm not sure I ever confirmed there was a weapon."

He returned her gaze, giving her a knowing smile. She knew it had been foolish to think that she could dupe him.

"Okay," she conceded. "On the basis that there may have been a particle beam weapon brought from Earth, something I can neither confirm nor deny, I have been told categorically by General Stockton that it is a tactical device placed here for defensive reasons only. And that is because our Chinese and Russian neighbors have done exactly the same thing and brought their own weapons."

"Which has pissed you off more. The fact that we now have weapons in contravention of all international laws or that you were lied to?"

"You know me too well, Joe. The military seems to be taking over and the politicians are paying attention. So much for a new start on Mars. And I knew absolutely nothing about any of this."

"Can't you prevent the weapons from being constructed and made operational?"

"How? If there's a viable way, please let me know."

Mancuso shrugged. "I imagine you'd need the agreement of all sides. Not very likely when trust is at an all-time low."

"Exactly. I've resigned myself to taking a back seat and hope the general and his advisers know what they are doing. But I will be ready to intervene if I have to. I have serious concerns that the situation will turn ugly."

"What about the Sentinels? Don't you think they'd step into to help?" suggested Mancuso.

Georgia moved to her favorite spot by the large window and sighed as she looked out at the plain disappearing into the distance. "No, we're being tested and judged by them. We're an interesting experiment, nothing more. They'll passively watch us blow ourselves up, make a few remarks on their notebook and move on to the next potential civilization. We're on our own. To be honest, I can now see the Sentinels' point. If they kept helping us out every time there was a chance of total annihilation, we would never learn from our mistakes. They'd be forever bailing us out."

"So, you're just going to stand there and do nothing, while the soldier boys turn this planet into a war zone. That doesn't seem like you."

Georgia didn't answer. Mancuso was right. She needed to do more. Somehow, she had let herself be convinced by Stockton and Bailey that the weapon was the right thing when she knew in her soul that it wasn't. She looked to the far distance and could just make out *Yorktown* at the end of the line of starships. Why wasn't she there now taking positive action. Instead she was making feeble excuses to Mancuso why she was allowing the weapon to be built.

***

Lieutenant Molloy completed a minuscule adjustment to the electron emitters. As he had suspected, there was a minor misalignment that could have caused degradation when the particle accelerator was switched on. He was now ready to join the captain and Paige for a short break before testing commenced. He was quietly thrilled to see what the weapon could actually do in field trials. If the computer predictions were accurate then a full power beam should be able to slice through rock like a knife through butter.

As he turned to walk toward the MEV, his peripheral vision caught a shimmering beam purple of light shine briefly onto the casing of the particle accelerator. The beam was narrow, maybe four inches across, and was oscillating. He noticed that whoever was controlling the beam was having problems with targeting and focus as it quickly darted from the particle weapon to the huge bulk of *Yorktown*, next to one of the landing fins. Behind that location was one of the fuel tanks for the main engines.

Molloy was instantly filled with panic. He understood instinctively what the beam was, even though it shouldn't be possible. "Captain," he shouted through his comms unit. "We're under attack. We need to get out of her now." Without hesitation, he sprinted toward the MEV, hoping they would have time to escape.

***

Captain Bailey stared out of the front window of the MEV as Molloy ran to the airlock. He spotted the beam directed at *Yorktown* and froze.

Beside him, Paige said. "That's impossible. There's no targeting technology that can provide that accuracy from orbit! It's impossible to compensate for the speed of the orbiting platform or changes in atmospheric conditions."

"There's no time to debate this now, Paige because we have visible proof that someone's achieved the impossible. We need to move away as soon as possible. Is Molloy on board?"

"Yes, he's in the airlock. How fast can this thing go?"

Bailey sat in the driver's seat to override the automatic controls. Deftly, he engaged reverse and felt the MEV begin to move.

"It's too late!" shouted Paige. She was watching the particle beam slice through the steel outer skin.

Bailey knew behind that location was one of the large fuel tanks. Although not full, there was probably still enough volatile fuel to cause significant damage if it ignited. The MEV would not protect them from the ensuing blast. What occurred next seemed to happen in slow motion. There was an explosion and a burst of bright orange flame erupted from the side of *Yorktown*. The explosion wasn't as intense as Bailey expected but then he watched with dread as the adjoining landing fin began to buckle. Its internal construction was compromised by the particle beam and had lost thee required rigidity. There was no way the three remaining fins could support the spaceship's weight and, as Bailey frantically looked up, he saw *Yorktown* begin to topple forward.

His right foot was already pushing the accelerator to the floor, but he applied more pressure in the vain hope of gaining more speed. Paige had now seen *Yorktown* falling in their direction and began to scream. Shutting out the noise, he opened a channel back to base. "Alpha, we're under attack. Please send help." That was all he was able to say before the full weight of *Yorktown* came crashing down on top of them.

***

Georgia and Mancuso stood in stunned silence as they watched from the control room as *Yorktown* fell slowly to the ground before being enveloped by a massive cloud of dust. Bailey's final message still rang in their ears.

"Joe, can you contact the MEV? We need to know what just happened out there."

Mancuso desperately tried all of the different comms channels, without success. "I'm sorry, Georgia," he said. "I can't reach any of them. All I'm picking up are other crew members calling in to report they saw *Yorktown* collapse."

Georgia took a few deep breaths to compose herself. What had Mac meant about being attacked? Who could have attacked *Yorktown* with such devastating effect?

"What do we do now?" asked Mancuso.

Without hesitation she replied. "We send out a rescue party. We have to believe there are survivors. I'll take Megan with me and two of *Lexington*'s crew. Issue a report to Ground Control. Let them know what's happened and how we're handling it."

"Is it wise to leave the base when we don't know more information about the attack?"

Georgia was already running toward the door. She glanced over her shoulder and said, "probably not. But I'm not leaving three people out there to die. Keep monitoring all channels and keep me updated." Before Mancuso could reply, she was gone.

***

In the control room on *Taipei*, General Zhang was less than happy. "What went wrong?" he demanded. "It took too long for the beam to be penetrate their ship. We should have been able to pick out a second target."

Liu squirmed in his seat at the unwanted attention. "After attacking the Russians, we weren't at full power. Also, you need to take account of the greater distance between us and the target. Perhaps the atmosphere dissipated some of the beam's energy. But you saw that we destroyed their ship and their weapon. The Americans will be defenseless next time our orbit is within range."

The explanation didn't improve Zhang's mood. "When will that be, colonel? I want to commence the next phase of our mission and establish our base on the surface. It has been too long since I felt the soil beneath my boots."

"I understand, general. I'm a sure the crew feels the same. Please give me a few moments to work out the calculations." Liu pulled up a different screen on the compute in front of him and keyed in some numbers. Conscious that the general was watching him closely, Liu swiftly came up with the answer. "We will not fly over Alpha Base for another eight orbits. We could be in position in six orbits if we use some fuel to perform a course correction."

General Zhang considered the options. "Do we have enough fuel for the course correction?"

Major Huang shook her head cautiously. "It would be inadvisable as we wouldn't be able to rendezvous with *Shandong* for a further two days. We don't have the supplies to last."

"In that case," continued Zhang, "we wait but we make our next shots count. Is that clear? I want the Americans obliterated from the planet. Inform *Shandong* what we are doing and instruct them to maintain their course"

Colonel Liu didn't relish spending the rest of the day in the cramped confines of *Taipei*'s control room, but the glory of the Republic of China was far superior than his own personal discomfort.

Chapter 23

Redmayne passed two bodies laying on the ground as he neared the airlock. Although their faces were constricted in agony, he recognized one of the Chinese scientists. Dark blotches on their skin evidence of where their blood had boiled in the ultra-low density atmosphere. He thought it likely they would have been alive for possibly thirty seconds after being sucked out onto the surface, their final moments a desperate yet agonizingly futile attempt to survive. Redmayne shivered at the thought that it could so easily be him lying there in the dust.

He could see where the roof of the command room was open to the elements. Shards of twisted metal rose into the air. Fragments of clothes had snagged on some of the metal and now hung limply. The roof was covered in debris. There was paper, chairs and even a computer console. They all revealed how catastrophic the explosion had been and made it all the more unlikely that anyone had survived.

Redmayne held his breath as he pressed the button to release the airlock door and was relieved to see the green light blink, allowing him to open the door. Stepping slowly inside, he noticed there was only emergency lighting. Taking a flashlight from a rack, he tried to open the inner door. There was some resistance and he had to push hard until there was a sufficient gap to squeeze through. His light revealed an oxygen tank had fallen and blocked the door. The whole corridor, in fact was littered with equipment and clothes. Cables were dangling from the ceiling and walls where the panels had been ripped off. It looked as if the base had been hit by a tornado.

He followed the corridor toward the control room, carefully stepping over the debris. The emergency lighting didn't offer much visibility, but his flashlight revealed enough. The further he walked into the base, the more evident that no one could have survived. The occupants had not expected the attack and there had been no time for anyone to act.

The former control room was unrecognizable. As the epicenter of the explosion, anything loose in the base whether it be clothes, furniture or people, had been sucked through the corridors, crashed into anything in its path before finally ripping through the roof. It was a total disaster zone. Equipment was destroyed or mangled, computer monitors shattered and a huge gaping hole looking up at the pale orange sky. Redmayne assumed that the power lines must have been cut in the explosion as none of the equipment appeared to be working. He found it surreal to see the room so dead when it was usually such a hive of activity. Under a fallen equipment rack were two more bodies on the floor. Redmayne knelt down in front of the first body and recognized it as Commander Koenig. The second was Romansky. Neither had stood a chance.

Redmayne carried on toward the living quarters. Safety doors that could have saved the crew were wide open. Two years of life on Mars has made us complacent, he thought. Such a waste of life that could have been avoided. Curtains, clothes, boots and personal effects littered the floors along with another three bodies. As Redmayne continued slowly forward, he knew his search was hopeless. He was the only one alive and the longer he remained in the base the more he was putting himself at risk of another attack.

Rounding a corner, he spotted a light coming from the emergency airlock. Against all hope, someone was in there. Redmayne hurried forward and looked through the glass window into the airlock. Inside was Professor Kozlovsky, who was sitting on a bench and sobbing. Redmayne tapped on the glass and pressed the intercom button, startling Kozlovsky. She looked up, wiping her red-rimmed eyes.

"My god!" she exclaimed. "I thought everyone was dead and I was going to die here alone. Are there any more survivors?"

"I don't think so," he replied. "I've only found you so far and the base is destroyed."

Anna started shaking uncontrollably. "What happened?"

"The base was attacked by an orbital particle weapon. I saw a beam aimed at the control room before there was a huge explosion caused by out gassing. I was at the solar farm when it happened."

"Who would do that?"

"I've been giving it some thought. It has to be the Chinese. I don't know why they did it but they're the only ones in orbit. It has to be them. How did you make it to safety?"

"Luck," she said quietly. "I was returning to my cabin after a shower when the decompression began and was next to this airlock. I thought it best to wait here to be rescued. Although I was beginning to wonder if anyone else had made it."

"I don't think it's a good idea to stay here. We need to get away before the base is attacked again. Is there a spare spacesuit in there?"

"Yes, but it's not my size. It looks like it was designed for a giant. I don't know if I can go outside. I'm scared."

Redmayne had sympathy for the traumas she was experiencing but he wasn't going to hang around. "I understand you're scared, Anna. But trust me it's not safe to stay here. We need to get to one of the landing craft and get away from here. You need to put the suit on now and come with me."

"I'm staying here. It's safer and we can wait for a rescue party."

"Who is going to rescue us. No one knows we're alive. There's no one on *Moskva* as everyone was at the base last night for the celebrations."

"What about the Americans? We can send them a distress call," Anna replied desperately.

"The comms here is smashed. The only way we can contact Alpha Base is from one of the landing craft. I don't think the Americans have the capability to reach us. Anna, our only chance is to get to the landing craft. So please move before it's too late. Otherwise, I'm leaving without you."

Anna considered her options before climbing into the spacesuit. Redmayne could see it was much too large for her and hoped that she would be able to move freely enough. It was a long walk to the *Kiev*.

***

Georgia led the way to *Yorktown* on her speeder, followed closely by Megan. The two *Lexington* crew members lagged a short way behind as they got used to driving on Mars. Georgia didn't wait for them as time was of the essence. She was focused on the crumpled smoking remains of *Yorktown*. Although the ship appeared to be substantially in one piece, its collapse had caused the thin metallic skin to squash and wrinkle. The damage was extensive, and she could see large areas where the skin had been torn or shredded. Long jets of vapor revealed where gases and liquids were escaping into the atmosphere, creating the potential for a fireball.

Georgia ignored the risk. She had to save the lives of the three astronauts trapped under the bulk of the spaceship. The closer she got, the more desperate her task looked. There was mangled wreckage everywhere. It was going to be difficult to locate the MEV. When she was less than two hundred yards from the wreckage, she slowed her speeder to walking pace and searched for any hint of the MEV or the astronauts. None of them were responding to her communications, which made the search all the more ominous.

Megan pulled up alongside her, shocked at the size of *Yorktown* now laying on its side. "I don't know how anyone could have survived that," she said. "It's like a vision from hell."

Georgia secretly agreed with her but said, "we don't give up until we find our colleagues. We can't make any assumptions until we know their fate for certain."

"That's fair enough, Georgia. But don't take any unnecessary risks. We don't want to lose anyone else."

"No one's lost yet," she replied angrily.

She continued her slow approach to what was left of *Yorktown* and began to move parallel to the ship, toward its tail. "There!" she exclaimed as she saw the rear of the MEV sticking out from *Yorktown*'s fuselage. The cab at the front of the MEV was completely hidden by wreckage but it looked as if the airlock at the rear was intact. Dismounting from her speeder, Georgia walked forward cautiously, looking for any signs of life. By now *Lexington*'s crew had pulled up next to Megan. They watched and waited for Georgia to say something.

As she moved closer, she could see that the MEV's chassis was buckled. The front axle looked as if it had collapsed under the weight of the spaceship which didn't bode well for the fate of the cab or anyone that may be inside. She stepped up to the airlock hatch and banged on it with her fist before resting her gloved hand flat on the door. Almost immediately, she felt three knocks in quick sensation. Someone was alive and inside.

"There's someone here," she shouted, excitedly. "I need some help."

The two crew members ran across to see what they could do. "The hatch won't open," Georgia said, calmer now that she knew there was at least one survivor. "The frame is buckled. We're going to have to force it open."

"But what if they're not wearing spacesuits?" said one of the crew. Georgia looked at his name badge.

"Larsson? We're just going to have to take that risk. Unless you have a better alternative."

"No, Ma'am I don't."

"The only way is to dismantle the hinges. So please get to it. We don't know how long we have. *Yorktown* is likely to be unstable and could collapse and there are numerous fuel leaks, just waiting for a spark to ignite."

It took two minutes for Larrson and his colleague to remove the locking pins for the hatch. They stepped back as whoever was inside the airlock forced the hatch open. Out stepped a beleaguered Lieutenant

Molloy, looking shaken and with blood running down the side of his head. Georgia peered inside the airlock, expecting to see Captain Bailey and Professor Duncan but the room was empty. Larsson helped Molloy step down from the MEV.

Georgia attached a comms cable to Molloy's suit so she could speak with him. "Molloy, where are the others?"

Molloy's face was grim as he replied. "They were inside the cab section and stood no chance when *Yorktown* came crashing down on top of us. I was in the airlock and saw them die!"

"Are you sure they're dead? Is there nothing we can do to rescue them?"

Molloy shook his head. "No, you'd be wasting your time. It was very quick is the only consolation I can give you."

"How could this have happened so quickly?" Georgia was struggling to accept that she'd lost another good captain. Although she'd only just started working with Bailey, she had been looking forward to working as his second in command. His sudden death was almost unbearable, but she knew she had other immediate priorities to take care of, the main one being no further loss of life against an unknown assailant.

"There was no warning. The intensity of the beam was sufficient to penetrate and melt the *Yorktown*'s steel supports. Do you know who did this to us?"

"I don't know," said Georgia, stunned by yet more deaths. "Tell me what happened."

"We were attacked by someone or something in orbit. I saw a particle beam targeted on *Yorktown* shortly before its destruction, the captain was trying to escape when there was a catastrophic failure in landing fin number two. After that, the ship toppled over on top of us. I'm surprised the fuel tanks haven't ruptured and caused a secondary explosion," he said in a monotone as he tried to process his experience.

Georgia studied the bulk of *Yorktown* with new concern. "We need to clear the area immediately because this ship could still blow. I want to recover the bodies, but they can wait. They're not going anywhere," she said bitterly.

With a new appreciation of the potential danger they were in, Georgia led the others away from *Yorktown*, back toward Alpha Base. But she was keen to get as much information from Molloy as she could.

"Did you see where the beam came from? Are we still imminent danger of another attack?" Georgia suddenly felt very exposed.

"The angle of the beam was low. My guess it was from an orbiting craft, just above the horizon to the north. Now I've had a few minutes to think about it, it has to be the Chinese. Somehow, they've developed the targeting system to fire accurately from space. We're still months away from having that technology on Earth. If whoever has that weapon is able to attack any point on the Martian surface, then they effectively control this planet. There is no defense and nowhere to hide."

"My worst-case scenario," she replied. *It made sense to knock out your enemies' weapons*, she thought, *notwithstanding a pre-emptive strike was an extreme and provocative act.* There had been no warning or advice from Ground Control. She looked back at the remains of the MEV and hoped that the end really had been swift for Mac and Professor Duncan. It wasn't going to be an easy task to retrieve their bodies and her immediate concern was the safety of the crew.

"Molloy, what can we do? I assume your particle beam weapon has been taken out of commission. Do you think Alpha is the next target?"

"Undoubtedly. If I was attacking an enemy, I'd make sure to attack their defenses before going for the main prize. There are several issues to consider. Our enemy will have limited periods to use their weapon against us. At standard orbital velocity, here's a maximum window of two minutes on each orbit when they're overhead. Although their orbital inclination means that they will not always have a clean line of sight or be in the optimal position. The location of Alpha means that the cliff face also offers some natural protection."

"That's more by luck than judgment," said Georgia, her mind racing with the various possibilities she was now facing. "Anything else I need to consider?"

"Particle beam weapons require a lot of energy. My best guess is that the Chinese are using solar powers to change battery packs. The energy storage capacity is finite and will need to be re-charged between firings."

"Can we determine when they are likely to attack next? And what their target will be?"

Molloy shook his head. "Not here. I need to get back to the base to work out their orbits. As for targets, it could be any of the ships or the base itself. Nowhere is safe now. I'm sorry to admit that your fears were correct."

"It's too late to worry about that now. We need to somehow protect the rest of the crew and perhaps evacuate the planet. I'll contact Mancuso to start the calculations. Let's return to base as quickly as we can. I know it's going to be precarious but you're going to have to share a speeder with Larsson."

Reluctantly, Georgia climbed back on her speeder and set off for Alpha Base with a heavy heart. Captain Bailey was a good man and didn't deserve to die like that. He wasn't sure how she was going to break the news to his crew. She hardly knew them yet now she had to tell them their captain had been killed and that they themselves were now targets. So much for stepping back from command decisions.

Chapter 24

By the time they reached *Kiev*, Anna had recovered much of her composure. She was in a state of shock from the extent of the damage inflicted on Derzost and had been horrified at witnessing her first dead bodies. She had recognized many colleagues she'd become close to on the *Moskva* and it was impossible to comprehend how their lives had ended so suddenly and violently. It was a terrible way to die.

With persuasion from Redmayne, her survival instincts had overridden her fear. She didn't want to die here on Mars. In fact, there was a growing part of her that wanted revenge for her fallen comrades. The attackers had been cowardly, and they needed to pay for their actions. She wasn't sure how, but she hoped that Redmayne would feel the same and have a cunning plan to assist her in dealing out retribution.

Anna was relieved to get inside *Kiev* and remove the over-sized spacesuit. The half mile walk had been the most uncomfortable in her life, the joints of the spacesuit rubbing her in the most awkward and intimate of places. She'd had to walk most of the way on tiptoe and her calves were now screaming in agony at the enforced exercise. She could also feel blisters on her left foot where it had rubbed inside the loose-fitting boot. "So, you've got us this far," she said. "What now?"

Some gratitude wouldn't go amiss, Redmayne thought. He had forgotten what it felt like for someone to rely on him. It was empowered and a huge weight had been lifted form those shoulders. His mind was now working overtime on rescuing the pair of them. "First, we check the fuel reserves. *Kiev* is always ready for emergency evacuation so it should be fully fueled to take us into orbit. The ship is semi-automated, and I have been shown the basic controls. We can then dock with *Moskva*, contact Moscow and advise them if our situation. After that, we stay out of the way of that particle beam until we can return to Earth."

They quickly climbed the steps from the airlock to the *Kiev*'s compact control deck which comprised eight metal seats surrounding a central console. The console contained two flight stations, for the commander and pilot, and was currently powered down. Redmayne flicked the power switch and a gentle hum could be felt through the deck plates as the console sprang into life. The two monitors began to show rows and rows of data as the main computer ran into diagnostics.

"How long do we have until the Chinese return?"

Checking his watch, he did a quick calculation in his head and said, "possibly thirty minutes. It depends on their orbit. Don't worry. The pre-launch check takes fifteen minutes, so we have time to spare."

"I hope you're right. We're sitting ducks at the moment."

Redmayne was well aware of that fact and hoped that he was right about the Chinese orbit. He wanted to be well away from the base before they returned to finish what they'd started.

***

After five minutes, Redmayne was able to confirm that the ship did indeed have enough fuel to reach an orbital velocity. But as each minute ticked by, the more conscious he became of the danger of a second attack. He'd noticed that Anna was sitting nervously staring blankly at the screens in front of her, no doubt reliving the trauma of the past hour. Part of him wanted to put a consoling arm around her but he decided it best she deal with her memories in her own way, at least for the time being. It looked as if they would be spending many months alone together and he didn't want to start off on the wrong foot. And he was grateful for the silence while he completed the complex pre-launch checks which he'd only ever watched being done.

They were both surprised when the comms channel suddenly burst into life. "Derzost. This is Georgia Pyke at Alpha Base. We have come under attack and sustained casualties. Commander Koenig, please can you confirm your status and if you can offer any assistance."

Redmayne had not heard Georgia's voice since he'd kidnapped her. She sounded as scared now as she had then. He recognized the slight tremor in her voice.

"The Chinese must have targeted the Americans as well," he said to Anna. "The attacks must have been carefully planned to be able to hit two locations within minutes."

"Unless it's a by the Americans. To trick us into thinking they are not responsible for the murder of our comrades." Anna's eyes were blazing with rage again.

"I don't think so. Georgia wouldn't do that. She's too honorable for her own good sometimes. She sounded genuinely afraid. You'll need to speak to her and explain our situation."

"Why not you? You know this Georgia Pyke."

"She thinks I've been dead for the past two years. I don't think she'll be very happy to hear my voice."

Anna muttered a curse under her breath that Redmayne could not hear. "Okay, I will do this. I'm not sure we can offer any assistance."

"Maybe not. But Alpha need to know we've been wiped out by the Chinese. Perhaps they can do something about it."

Anna nodded and reluctantly put on the headset. "Alpha Base. This is Professor Anna Kozlovsky, chief scientist at Derzost. About one hour ago our base was also attacked. I believe it was from an orbiting particle beam weapon. We were taken by surprise and there is only one survivor other than me. Twenty-eight people are presumed dead and the base is destroyed."

There was a twenty second pause before Georgia's voice could be heard again. "I am truly sorry for your loss Professor Kozlovsky. It seems as if we have a common enemy. I have informed my government and am awaiting instruction. What are your immediate intentions?"

"Our main comms were destroyed in the attack, so no one knows what has happened to us. We are currently on our landing craft and will be taking off shortly to return to *Moskva*. I do not want to be here when the Chinese make their next pass. They have already shown they have no mercy."

***

Georgia was stunned by the Russian professor's news. It sounded as if their base had taken a greater hit. The loss of life was deliberate and unimaginable. Whoever had ordered the attacks had ruthlessly disabled both bases in one swoop, eradicating any chance of defense or resistance. Was there going to be an invasion? Were their lives in jeopardy?

She turned to Molloy and Mancuso who were standing next to her in the control center. They both looked pale at what they had just heard. "Thoughts anyone?" she asked out of desperation.

Molloy replied, "The Chinese now have a clear tactical advantage. They've virtually wiped out the Russians and there is little doubt they will do the same to us as soon as they get the opportunity. The planet is basically theirs. We have no one to come to our rescue. In two years, when the next Expeditions arrive, the Chinese could have made this planet impregnable. We need to somehow stop them."

"How do you suggest we do that?" said Mancuso, trying hard to control his anger.

"I don't know if our weapon was destroyed in the attack," said Molloy, trying to recall what had happened. "We could be lucky. The direction *Yorktown* fell means the weapon may have survived. And I recognize Professor Kozlovsky's name. She and her team have been carrying out similar research on particle beam technology. If you can get her here, she may be able to help us."

Georgia pressed the comms button. "Professor. We have an alternative suggestion for you. Are you able to perform a suborbital flight to Alpha Base instead? We may be able to defeat the Chinese with our own particle weapon and avenge your fallen colleagues. However, we require your expertise. I know it's a lot to ask of you but if we don't give it a try then we're as good as handing Mars over to the Chinese."

***

Redmayne wasn't expecting the request from the Americans. The countdown clock showed less than five minutes until *Kiev* was ready for launch and return to the relative safety of the orbiting mother ship. Georgia's suggestion was ridiculous.

"How do they know who I am?" Anna asked.

"They'll have files on everyone here. The same as you have detailed records of the American and possibly Chinese astronauts. It's nothing to be concerned about."

"That is true," conceded Anna. "The Americans have a Professor Duncan leading their weapons program. She is very proficient but not as good as me. Maybe she has finally realized my skills are superior to hers. That is why they want my assistance."

"I'm not sure it's wise to go. We're so close to launch. We can be on board *Moskva* in under four hours."

"I agree. Although I do not like running away after what the Chinese did to us, the risk while we stay on the planet is too great. It would take me days, if not weeks, to understand Professor Duncan's work. She should know that."

"In that case, we decline the offer and get out of here," said Redmayne.

Anna nodded and switched the comms to transmit. "I'm sorry Miss Pyke. I doubt I can offer any more than Professor Duncan can give you. We're heading to *Moskva* in four minutes and I suggest you also take your ships to orbit before the next strike."

Georgia's reply was immediate. "Professor Duncan was killed in the unprovoked attack, along with Captain Bailey. I wouldn't ask if the was another way. I hate running away without retaliation. If we evacuate, then we lose the planet. I've invested far too much of my life here to be bullied out. We're currently calculating the Chinese vessels orbit but we think we may have time to set up our own weapon as a defense. Fly here and if you can't help us then you still have time to escape, possibly with some of my crew."

Anna cut the link and glanced at Redmayne. "What do you think? Part of me believes we should help, and it sounds as if we have nothing to lose."

Redmayne scowled back. Conflicted by Georgia's impassioned plea, his first instinct was to get into orbit as soon as possible. Going to Alpha increased his risk. If the Chinese didn't get him then the Americans certainly would once they discovered his existence. "I have everything to lose. I can't go back to Alpha Base. They'll arrest me on sight. We don't know for sure we wouldn't still be an immediate target for the Chinese either."

Anna wouldn't have any of his excuses. Her anger had grasped the possibility of a plan for revenge. "Maybe you should see it as an opportunity to wipe the slate clean. They need my help to defeat the Chinese. We can use that as a bargaining tool in order to give you a second chance. The alternative is you return to Russia with me. I don't think that will be a pleasant experience either."

"When you put it that way, maybe you're right." If the previous two years were anything to go by, he would continue to be despised when he returned to Earth. Surviving when so many cosmonauts had died would not change that perception. "Pass me the radio," he said resignedly.

As Anna handed over the headset, Redmayne felt physically sick. After two years of secrecy, was he doing the right thing declaring his presence. What would the reaction be? He was, yet again, being forced into making difficult decisions. His hand hesitated over the control button that would commit him to a new path. Sensing Anna was watching him, he found a small glimmer of resolve and pressed the button.

"Georgia, this is Tom Redmayne. I'm the only other survivor of the attack. I think we need to talk."

***

There was utter disbelief in Alpha's control room. The sound of Redmayne's voice brought back so many dark suppressed memories for Georgia that she was temporarily overwhelmed. A chill passed through her. Part of her had always suspected he had survived their last encounter although she'd never had any evidence to support that. Until now.

She looked at Mancuso who returned her gaze. She knew he'd been just as deeply affected by Redmayne's previous actions, although had repressed any emotions of anger and sadness. At least she'd had Megan as support during the strenuous months following the deaths of Commander Anders and Captain Winter at Redmayne's hands.

"Trust you to turn up now, Redmayne. Have you got anything to do with these attacks?" She hoped that the resentment and bitterness she felt was adequately conveyed in her voice.

"I'm sure you're not pleased to hear from me again after all this time, but I promise I am a victim on this occasion."

"I find that hard to believe. But then I stopped trusting you a long time ago. When you murdered my captain!"

"There's no time to live in the past Georgia. Not if you want to defeat the Chinese. I'm currently on the *Kiev* with Anna. She's prepared to help you, but she needs me to pilot the ship to your location. You can see my quandary with this. You'll lock me up as soon as I land. I need an incentive to make the risk worth my while."

"Putting yourself first as always. Two years with the Russians hasn't changed you. What do you want?"

"Amnesty in return for delivering Professor Kozlovsky. I don't expect forgiveness, Georgia. I truly regret my actions and the deaths I caused. I can't change what happened but perhaps I have a chance now to show you I'm not the evil villain you think I am. Allow me to help defend the planet."

Georgia angrily hit the mute button. "Molloy. How much to you need the Professor's help?"

"I don't know the extent of the damage to the particle accelerator. She's the only other person with the knowledge to test it with me."

Mancuso had started drumming his fingers rhythmically on the desk as soon as he heard Redmayne's voice. "There has to be another way," he said. "You cannot seriously be considering having that twisted murderer back here. He needs to be judged for what he did."

"Joe, I am as repulsed as you are that he's still alive. But suddenly we have more important issues to contend with. Do you have any alternatives because I'd much rather go with a plan that doesn't include Redmayne?" Georgia still found it extremely challenging to make compromises in order to achieve the bigger picture. At times like this she always considered what Captain Winter would do when faced with the same facts. It made the decision-making process slightly easier, even when she still wasn't convinced she'd made the correct choice.

Joe looked as helpless as she felt inside. He sat in his chair and said nothing.

She hit the transmit button again. "Okay Redmayne. It looks as if fate has brought us together again. I give you my word that you will be free to leave this base once the Chinese threat has been dealt with. But you will be escorted at all times when you are here. Is that acceptable?"

"It is, coming from you," Redmayne replied. "It will several minutes for me to reprogram your coordinates into the flight computer. We should arrive within the hour."

"Don't make me regret this, Redmayne." Georgia cut the transmission already filled with a sense of foreboding. She turned slowly toward Mancuso. "This is on me, Joe. I'll break the news to Megan."

Chapter 25

Georgia found Megan in the medical center, updating some data on her computer. Doctor Coleman was sitting across from her, silently typing away on his own computer. Georgia could sense the tension in the room between. It was going to take a long time for the doctors to resolve their differences.

"Sorry to interrupt. Megan, I need a word with you in private."

Megan smiled and immediately stood, seemingly pleased for an excuse to leave the room. "Yes, of course. What can I help you with?"

Georgia led the way down the corridor and outside into the open cave area before she spoke. "You probably don't want to hear this. Redmayne's alive and still on Mars!" She turned to face Megan to see the reaction, which was a mix of shock and surprise.

"How do you know? Are you sure?"

"I just spoke with the bastard. As we suspected, the Russians have been looking after him. But Derzost was also attacked this morning and he's one of only two survivors."

"That figures," groaned Megan. "That man seems to have nine lives. So, the attacks were coordinated."

"I spoke with a Russian scientist. She is convinced it's the Chinese. And I have to agree with her. There's one more thing you need to know. I've invited the Russian and Redmayne here. They'll be arriving in their landing craft shortly."

"Seriously? You're allowing him to return?"

"I didn't have a choice. We need the scientist's expertise on particle beams. But she doesn't know how to pilot their craft. What would you have me do?"

"I hope you're going to seize him as soon as he lands. He should be made to pay for his murders."

Georgia had a lot sympathy for her best friend's views. She wanted to see Redmayne punished as much as anyone else. "I'm sorry. I promised that he could leave once the threat has been dealt with. He wouldn't have come otherwise."

Tears formed in Megan's eyes. "Why would you do this after all the anguish he's caused? How can you trust him?"

Georgia put her arm reassuringly around Megan's shoulders. "I don't trust him. You saw what the Chinese did to *Yorktown*. They've destroyed Derzost. We're defenseless here and need all the help we can get. I've done the deal for pure practical reasons. To try and save our lives."

Megan stared coldly back. "The price is too high." And with that she walked back inside the complex, just as Jackson was stepped out.

"Hey sis, I just heard about the Russian base. Does that mean we're not safe here?"

Georgia was deflated following her brief conversation with Megan. The unexpected events of the day were beginning to overwhelm her. "I don't know," she replied tiredly. "It's highly likely but I don't know why the Chinese are attacking. A motive would be useful."

"In that case, shouldn't we be evacuating?"

"*Lexington* is being refueled but that will take about twelve hours. I don't know if we have that much time. And I'm not ready to leave this planet until I have to."

"The joys of command," Jackson said dryly.

"I thought I'd handed all responsibility to Captain Bailey. I guess this is another challenge I need to face head on. I need to get back to the control center." Reluctantly, Georgia started walking toward the front of the base, her feet feeling like lead weights.

"I'm here for you, sis. Let me know if there's anything I can do," called out Jackson.

***

"How did Megan take the news?" Mancuso asked as soon as Georgia walked back into the control center.

"Not as well as you," she replied. Seeing that the room was empty, she asked, "Where's Molloy?"

"Preparing to head back to *Yorktown* to assess how safe it is and to view any possible damage to the particle weapon. Even if *Yorktown* missed the weapon, there's bound to be some damage or recalibration required. He's taking Rashid with him. You've also received a reply from General Stockton."

"Okay. Play the message."

An image of Stockton appeared on the main screen, with NASA Administrator Walter Dexter sitting next to him. Both men had grave expressions etched across their faces. Stockton spoke first. "Georgia, we've received your report with a sense of disbelief and sorrow. Firstly, let me pass on our commiserations for the sudden loss of Captain Bailey and Professor Duncan in what can only be described as a despicable attack. We have advised the families and I'm sure you can imagine their responses. We immediately informed President Wyndham who in turn has contacted the Chinese government to express his outrage in no uncertain terms. He considers the aggression an act of war. The matter is currently being debated by Congress in closed session. No decision has yet been made on what we tell the public. The knowledge that we've taken weapons to Mars is clearly bound to be a sensitive issue, but we cannot deny that two of our astronauts have been brutally murdered."

Administrator Dexter continued. "That's where things become really complicated. The Chinese official statement is that there has been an unfortunate accident with its spacecraft. Privately, however, they have told us they've lost control of the situation aboard the *Shandong*. There appears to have been a mutiny. A General Zhang has taken command after the captain of the *Shandong* met with a sudden and tragic accident. Since then, Beijing has not been able to make contact with their crew who they think have gone rogue. To be honest, we're not sure if China is telling the truth. Our analysts are continuing to assess the situation."

"We've also spoken with Moscow," said Stockton. "They have their own worries as contact with Derzost was suddenly lost less than two hours ago. It seems more than just a coincidence that this event occurred about twenty minutes before the attack on *Yorktown*. My best guess is that you were the secondary target. Zhang is taking out any possible threats on the planet, which makes it highly likely he will be coming back to finish the job. You've seen first-hand what their beam is capable of. It can penetrate the walls of Alpha Base, so you and the crew are not safe. If you've not already done so, you need to implement evacuation procedures. We will continue to push for a diplomatic solution at this end but, if China are telling the truth, I hold out little hope of preventing Zhang from firing again on Alpha."

"Your safety is of paramount importance," added Dexter. "Do whatever you have to do to save the crew and keep us informed of any news."

"I second that, Georgia," said Stockton. "Don't take any risks. We'll continue to do everything at this end to resolve matters with China. But get the crew safe. We can replace the base. We can't replace you or the crew."

Georgia paused the message. "Joe, when will *Lexington* be fueled and ready for take-off?"

"At least eleven hours. All pumps at the propellant depot are at maximum output already. *Lexington* was running on fumes by the time it landed so we have a lot of tank to fill. In any event, we need that time to stock the ship with enough supplies to get us back to Earth."

"Will extra manpower make a difference?"

"It may shave off thirty minutes. Vicky Morris is doing a great job with help from the crew."

"Joe, can you offer your assistance to. Your load master experience is invaluable, and we need it now. Do what you can to get the minimal supplies loaded."

"I'm on it." Mancuso jumped up and ran toward the airlock.

Georgia slumped into a chair and took a long look out of the window. Beyond, she could see evidence of activity. Clouds of dust were being kicked up by speeders and robotic crawlers towing trailers laden with pallets. She could just make out *Lexington's* empty cradle slowly being lowered to the ground, awaiting its next load of supplies.

It was now midday and the sun was at its highest. She estimated they had another five hours before the sun set behind the cliff face. Working in the darkness and freezing temperatures would bring its own dangers and slow down the progress. But there was still hope that Professor Kozlovsky and Lieutenant Molloy could make the particle beam operational. She was determined to show General Zhang that she had some teeth as well and that Mars would not be an easy prize to obtain.

Turning back to the computer monitor she began to record an update for General Stockton, wondering if he would approve of her deal with Redmayne. She wasn't even sure if she approved of it but, then, Dexter had told her to do whatever she has to do to save the crew.

Chapter 26

Kiev landed with a resounding thud less than two hundred yards from *Lexington*. Redmayne killed the rocket motors one second too soon, causing the landing craft to bounce into the air before settling in a cloud of dust. He sheepishly looked across at Anna, who was looking pale as she gripped tightly to the arms of her chair. "I'm sorry about that," he said, shrugging his shoulders. "I should have mentioned I've only landed this craft once and never had proper training."

"You decide to tell me this now?" she said, grateful that she hadn't just died.

"You may not have flown if I'd told you the truth," he replied with a mischievous smile.

"No, I wouldn't have. You landed very close to the Americans' ship."

Redmayne laughed. "Yes, I saw some of their astronauts running for cover. They were more afraid than you were. I wanted to be close to their refueling rig so that we can make our escape." He pressed the comms button in front of him. "Alpha, we've landed. What are your instructions?"

Georgia replied immediately. "I watched your approach. I don't think you'll be getting any awards for that landing. Head over to the *Lexington* next to you. It's the one you almost shunted! We have some speeders there. Redmayne, I want you back here with me where I can see you. Professor Kozlovsky, one of my crew will accompany you straight to *Yorktown* where you will find Lieutenant Molloy assessing the viability of our particle accelerator. Time really is of the essence here as we now know what we're up against."

Both Redmayne and Anna unstrapped themselves and made their way to the airlock in silence. Redmayne noticed that Anna was more relaxed after finding a spacesuit that was close enough to her size to be comfortable. He, on the other hand, was feeling extremely nervous as he checked his air supply and put on his helmet. He was going into the lion's den and, not for the first time, was wondering if it had been wise to return to Alpha. With a growing sense of foreboding, he sealed the inner airlock and started the decompress sequence.

***

The first thing Redmayne noticed as they approached *Lexington* on foot was the number of astronauts busily moving pallets from one place to another. This was a controlled evacuation in the event that the main plan was unsuccessful. Despite Georgia's earlier fighting talk, she was hedging her bets. It was wise to have a fall back but how much time was it going to take to prepare the ship for a return to Earth?

He then saw Joe Mancuso, standing next to three speeders and staring at him intently. "I really hoped you had died, Redmayne," he sneered, not trying to hide any hatred. "You have no right to be here after what you did."

Redmayne moved forward cautiously. "I understand how you must feel, Joe. Nothing I can say will change that, but I am here to assist Georgia in order to defeat our mutual enemy. Let me introduce you to Professor Anna Kozlovsky."

Mancuso softened his gaze as he looked at Anna. "It's a pleasure to meet you, professor, although I wish it were under different circumstances. My name is Joe Mancuso and I'm here to escort you to *Yorktown*"

Anna returned his gaze before looking doubtfully at the speeders. "Thank you, Mister Mancuso. I have never ridden one of these devices. You will need to show me."

Mancuso nodded. "You can call me Joe. They're easy to use and I'll give you a crash course in five minutes." His frown darkened as he looked back at Redmayne. "You know how to use these. I suggest you get out of my sight as quickly as you can. Georgia will be waiting for you. Do everything she tells you because, if you piss me off, I won't be responsible for the consequences."

Although Redmayne was over six foot and physically strong, he had no doubt that Mancuso would make short work of him if provoked. Without saying another word, he jumped onto the nearest speeder and set off for Alpha Base, relieved to be creating distance between Mancuso and himself.

***

Redmayne stepped out of the airlock with his helmet under his arm, ready for a frosty welcome. He wasn't disappointed. Georgia was leaning against the far wall, her arms crossed, staring defiantly at him. "I've been told letting you in is a big error of judgment. Don't prove me wrong. And don't for one minute think I'm happy that you're still alive."

He nodded in absolute agreement. "Georgia, I understand that I'm here solely because of a mutual threat. And I'm more than aware you left me for dead two years ago. Your Sentinel friends may have played mind tricks with me that cause me the odd nightmare, but I am grateful that you didn't kill me when you had the chance. You're clearly a better person than I am."

"I don't need your speeches either. Follow me." Georgia turned went through a door and up two flights of steps that led into the control center. She moved to her spot near the window and stared out at the view while Redmayne took a seat. "I assume you were involved in the Russian's weapons research program," she said.

"Actually, you're wrong," he replied. "I found out yesterday when I was enlisted to assist Professor Kozlovsky. I have only a rudimentary knowledge of how the particle beam weapon works. I thought having the weapon here was a bad idea, but it wasn't for me to say."

Georgia considered his response for a moment. "After this morning's events it seems we were both correct to be concerned. Apparently, the attacks were undertaken by a rogue Chinese general. There was a mutiny on the *Shandong* and their captain was killed. The Chinese leadership claim they have no knowledge of the attacks and cannot contact their own vessel."

"That's rather careless," said Redmayne, immediately regretting his flippancy. "So, we're faced with an out of control fanatic. Do you know what he wants?"

"Not yet. I'm waiting for further information and instructions from Earth."

As she spoke, the computer in front of Redmayne pinged to indicate a message had been received. Georgia walked across and saw the message was from General Stockton. She hesitated before pressing the play button, undecided as to whether Redmayne should listen in. But there was no time to waste moving him to another room. In theory he was her prisoner and she could still hold him on the base if he learned too much.

This time, General Stockton was alone. "Thanks for your latest update," he began. "I'm as dismayed as you that the bastard Redmayne is still alive. It proves once again why we can't trust the Russians. I understand why you did what you felt you had to do to get Professor Kozovsky to Alpha. Do not let that evil fucker out of your sight for one moment. And remember, everyone thinks he's dead so, if he has an accident of any kind, he won't be missed and there will be no action taken against you." He said this final statement with a twisted smile.

Georgia winced and paused the message before glancing at the smiling Redmayne. "I don't suppose you weren't supposed to hear that," she said. "But now you know how well thought of you are on Earth."

Redmayne continued to smile. "I don't think you'd see me harmed. I promise not to test you though. I'm surprised that Stockton is still going though. Surely he's way past retirement age and should be bothering old women on cruises around the Caribbean!"

Georgia ignored him and pressed the play button again to continue the message from Stockton.

"We've received more information from China, which we believe is genuine. General Zhang is in his seventies and is highly decorated. Apparently, he's been disenchanted for some time with how the Chinese have engaged the West, especially with expansion into the South China Sea. He's a member of a faction that wants China to be more assertive and expand its sphere of influence. It seems he's taken it upon himself to claim Mars for China, eradicating any other nations that may be inhabiting the planet. Somehow, he even managed to recruit some of his most loyal staff to the mission, which must have made the mutiny so much easier. The Chinese government does not condone this action. At least that's what they're telling us.

"Satellite imagery has confirmed the destruction of Derzost. We advised Moscow of your previous report and the information provided by Redmayne. They have privately made political approaches to China and want Zhang and his crew returned to Earth to face punishment. That seems unlikely if China is actually telling the truth.

"The bottom line is that General Zhang is definitely coming for Alpha Base. It will take only a few well-placed shots to disable the base or destroy *Lexington* and then he can pick you off at will, or let you die a slow lingering death. With Beijing unable to contact Zhang and his supporters there is absolutely nothing we can do from here. I'm sorry, but you're on your own. You're fully authorized to use our weapon against Zhang's ship. I hope, for your sake, that the weapon was not damaged in the previous attack. The Chinese are well aware of our intent and are not raising any objections. They've also confirmed your calculations regarding Zhang's orbit and when he'll next be in range.

"All I can do now is wish you good luck and pray for the safety of your crew. I have the utmost faith in each and every one of you. Stockton out."

"So we created an ultimate weapon and put in the hands of a madman," Redmayne muttered. "Perhaps we shouldn't survive as a species. We're too stupid for our own good."

"It's a handful of people, like you Redmayne, that put everyone's lives in jeopardy. Why can't we all think about big picture? Does no one want to find out what the Universe has in store for us?" Georgia slammed her fist in frustration. She wanted to say *I told you so* to the general, but it was too late for that.

"Georgia, take it from someone who knows," said Redmayne softly. "That handful of people succeed because they're ruthless and afraid. I was scared when I lost Laura Banstead on Expedition One that I'd never find anyone like her again. Over time, that feeling turned into hatred and then into a thirst for revenge. I chose the wrong path but was blinded by my rage. It doesn't matter if you believe me, but I am truly sorry for what I did. The politicians, generals and scientists that create these weapons or decide on starting wars are afraid of change or the unknown. Across generations, they've learned the best form of defense is attack. Somewhere along the way they lost their humanity. As I did. But I now recognize that fact. Sometimes the best people make mistakes but only the strong survive to write the history books."

Georgia was surprised by Redmayne's honesty and clarity. It brought a tear to her eye which she quickly brushed away. "That's what I'm seeking to regain here. Our humanity. There's no place for weapons. Once we destroy Zhang, I'll be dismantling our own particle beam weapon. Stockton won't like it, but he won't have a say."

"You'll need to fire at Zhang's ship before he gets a chance to use his weapon. Do you think that's possible?"

"Let's see what the experts have to say."

***

The news from the experts wasn't good. Thirty minutes later, Molloy reported in on his way back to the base with Rashid and Anna.

"I'm sorry Georgia, it's bad news. Initially we all believed we could get it working. There was no real obvious sign of damage and we were able to get power to the particle accelerator. It was only then that we discovered the copper tubes and microwave generators are completely misaligned. They must have been hit pretty hard by debris. It will take months for me to repair them. The weapon is as good as obsolete."

Georgia hid the dismay she was feeling. "Thank you for trying, Molloy. We knew it was a possible long shot after the *Yorktown*'s destruction. Hurry back and you can all assist with the evacuation."

She turned off the comms channel and slumped in her chair, not caring that a few tears ran down her cheek.

Jackson had just joined Georgia and Redmayne in the control center. He went up to her and gently put his arms around his sister. "It's not your fault. No one saw this coming or knew that Zhang was a megalomaniac. Leaving this planet isn't a failure. You should see it as giving everyone a chance to live."

Georgia patted his hand. "Good try, Jacko. I don't see it that way. This is my home and I'm being forcibly evicted. It doesn't sit well with me. You're right about one thing though. My priority is now the safety of the crew. The problem is we don't have enough time before Zhang is able to attack us again."

Redmayne interrupted her thought process. "From my limited understanding, Zhang only has enough power to fire the weapon for twenty to thirty seconds before he needs to recharge. And he's only in range for several minutes on each orbit. So, he can't destroy this base and all the ships in one single pass. That gives us some hope of more time."

"Does it?" replied Georgia. "What will he target next? Does he go straight for the base, or *Lexington*, or the propellant factory? The base seems a logical start as he can destroy communications, living quarters and our means of survival. But if I take a gamble by putting the crew on *Lexington*, who's to say he won't fire on that first? Or on his next orbit?"

"Have you thought about negotiating with Zhang?" suggested Jackson.

"What do you mean? He's shown no hint of wanting to talk so far," said Georgia.

"I don't see what you have to lose. Try to contact him. Ask him for more time to make preparations to leave Mars. There doesn't need to be any more bloodshed. He lets us head back to Earth peacefully and he can have the base intact as a prize. At least you'll discover if he has any compassion whatsoever."

While Georgia gave it some consideration, Redmayne said, "It won't work. I like the idea, but Zhang's consistent actions so far show he doesn't know the meaning of mercy. He only wants to demonstrate the might of the weapon and of China."

"I hate to admit it but Redmayne's probably right," said Georgia. "But I can't rule out any options as the moment. I have twenty-four lives to think about."

Chapter 27

General Zhang knew he was becoming increasingly irritable. He only had a vague understanding of the complex physics of orbital mechanics, relying on experts around him to explain whatever he needed to know. He now wished he'd taken more time reading up on the subject. Colonel Liu had spent some time explaining the niceties around energy conservation requirements for altering trajectories and altitude of fast moving objects around a sphere, but he still didn't grasp the reasons why it was taking the *Taipei* so many orbits to be back over Alpha Base.

He had tried to sleep in his seat, but the constant annoying hum of the computers and environmental systems were too loud to shut out. More frustrating was the fact that Colonel Liu and Major Huang didn't seem affected by the noise and had quickly fallen asleep. If he couldn't sleep, then no one else should be able to.

"It is no time to rest," he said, loudly, startling his two officers. "We must ensure that the weapon is operational, the targeting computer ready and the batteries are full capacity. There will be no excuses this time."

Huang took several seconds to wake properly from what had been a deep sleep. "General, the batteries will be at full capacity within three hours. Plenty of time before Alpha is back in range. We will destroy the base. There is no doubt that will happen."

"In that case we should alter our trajectory further so that we reach the target sooner. One less orbit will save us eighty minutes."

"For what purpose?" asked Liu. "Alpha Base isn't going anywhere. We'll burn more propellant and move us in the opposite direction to *Shandong*. Our fuel levels would be at a critical level. I'm not sure it's worth the risk."

"I agree with the Colonel," said Huang. "The course we're on gets us above Alpha in the minimum time using the maximum safe amount of propellant. We have the advantage over the Americans. Why jeopardize our success?"

"I don't need to explain myself," shouted Zhang. He didn't appreciate his orders being questioned. "I don't want to give the Americans the chance to regroup now that they know we're here. It's a basic military principle to destroy your enemy swiftly and decisively."

"I understand that, general. You taught us well, many years ago," Liu replied, staying calm. He appreciated it would make matters worse if he confronted General Zhang. "You saw what we did to their ship and their feeble weapon. The base is defenseless, and the Americans are panicking. War in space is different to back on Earth when we faced our enemies head on in ground attacks. We no longer see the fear in our enemy's eyes or smell the blood and gore of battle. We must learn a new patience and wait for the opportunity to come to us. Your victory will still be glorious, and you will be a hero."

Zhang listened, trying to control his anger. Colonel Liu was an accomplished and trusted soldier and had yet to fail him. If anyone had spoken to him the way Liu just had, they would have been swiftly dispatched through the nearest airlock. He had studied the hardest for this mission and was the best tactical officer in the Chinese army. Which meant that he was probably correct in his assessment of the situation. The ultimate goal was within striking distance. What did it matter if it took them slightly longer?

His thoughts were interrupted by Major Huang. "General. *Shandong* has informed me that they're received a transmission. Someone is requesting to speak directly with you."

"If it's Beijing again then we continue to maintain communications blackout until all targets have been destroyed. I don't want the crew distracted by ignorant political officers telling them they are traitors to the country."

"No, it's from the commander of the American base."

"Begging for mercy, no doubt. The Americans are nothing but cowards when they have their weapons taken away. I will speak with them. They should know who has defeated them in battle. Establish a link."

***

In Alpha Base's control center, Georgia held her breath as she waited to hear whether General Zhang would speak with her. Megan had just arrived stood at the back of the room, staring uncomfortably at Redmayne. She had previously studied in Shanghai for two years and understood some basic Mandarin and was there in case any translation was required. The atmosphere in the room was tense and silent. Everyone was acutely aware this could be the last attempt to save themselves and the crew.

After several minutes of waiting, they heard a voice in broken English say through the loudspeaker, "I am Colonel Liu Haipeng on board the CS *Taipei*. I understand you wish you speak to General Zhang Zhen."

Out of habit, Georgia leaned forward into the microphone, " Hello Colonel Liu. I am Georgia Pyke, acting commander of Alpha Base. I would like the general to explain the reasons for his unprovoked attack on this facility, the destruction of Derzost and the unnecessary loss of life."

There was a long pause during which time Georgia began to worry she had been too direct. She glanced nervously at Megan who shrugged her shoulders. After fifteen seconds, a different, older sounding voice, finally spoke.

"Commander, my name is General Zhang. I am claiming Mars on behalf of the People's Republic of China. To that end, it is necessary to remove all other inhabitants. The attacks were necessary to neutralize the weapons that could have been used to prevent my mission. I make no excuses for the inevitable loss of life."

"General, the Chinese president is denying any knowledge of your actions. He has told our government you have taken it solely upon yourself and have no authority for what you have done. I therefore request you cease any further attacks and talk with your government."

"You are misinformed. The Chinese leadership is weak, but they will fully support my actions once my mission here is complete."

"That sounds as if you intend further attacks. You already destroyed our only weapon and killed several of my colleagues. There is no need for further bloodshed. This planet is big enough for our nations to co-exist peacefully." Georgia wasn't convinced her words were getting through. She stared out of the viewing window at the astronauts busily preparing *Lexington*. The knowledge she was responsible for each of those lives was weighing heavily on her.

"I think you'll find that the governments on Earth have demonstrated how difficult it is for two different ideologies to live and work together. We have faced many years of sanctions from the West, designed to cripple and hamper our economic growth. We have been restricted from extending our borders. We are accused of human rights violations by countries who hide the atrocities they carry out on their own citizens. It is time to stop the toleration of hypocrisy and discrimination against my country. China will rise again. Unfortunately, you won't see it."

Georgia flicked the mute button and looked around the room. "Definitely a crazed fanatic! Any suggestions?"

Jackson replied, "I've not read any books for dealing with a nut job! He has deep seated views that you're not going to change."

"Agreed," said Redmayne. "The general is blinkered. He's probably had many years to build up excuses for his beliefs. He has convinced himself and those around him that he has justification for the path he has chosen to take. You'll never change that now."

"But does he have any shred of compassion?" asked Georgia. "Something I can use to let us leave the planet safely?"

"No," replied Megan, coldly. "He's here to conquer. That's all he's focused on. He doesn't care about loss of life." She was staring at the back of Redmayne's head as she said it with a depth of feeling that took Georgia by surprise.

Feeling deflated, Georgia re-opened the comms channel. "General, I understand you want the planet but there are better ways of handling it. There's no need for further military action. We will cause you no harm and will leave peacefully at the end of our current deployment."

She could hear the general laughing. "I don't think so, acting commander. Politicians have had their chances. The only way is taking decisive action. I've lived long enough to know that politics and compromise works in no one's favor. Your wasting your time and mine if you think otherwise. I think I've answered your question. There's nothing more to be said."

"Wait!" Georgia said desperately. "It is clear that you are a very powerful man and hold all of the cards. Allow us to leave and we'll hand over this base to you. No tricks. Give us eight hours to load *Lexington* and we will leave Mars. Alpha Base is established. It has power, water and everything that you need. You don't need to destroy it or kill us. Show some compassion and I'm sure it will go a long way to healing relationships between our countries."

"You've not listened to me. I have no need for compassion. The actions of your country and those that align with it have taken that from me. I do not need your base or supplies. We have brought everything we need to establish our own outpost. I want to set an example of China's greatness that will send shudders through all of our adversaries and put fire in the blood of my people once again. You have four hours to leave. Our conversation is at an end acting commander."

Megan let out a deep breath. "That went as expected. No, we know for sure we're screwed."

Georgia ignored and said, "Redmayne, what about the landing craft you traveled here on? Is there enough fuel to get to orbit?"

"Possibly. We used some fuel for the sub-orbital transit and the tanks were full before we left. But there's only room for ten people, twelve at a push. There won't be fuel or time for two trips. Plus, *Moskva* isn't stocked with supplies or fuel to return that many people to Earth. We'd be stranded in orbit until the supplies ran out or General Zhang finds us."

"It gives twelve people a chance of surviving though," said Megan. "It's more than any of us have at the moment. It's worth considering."

Jackson agreed. "It will provide hope to those dozen people. Perhaps *Moskva* can act as a lifeboat until help arrives from Earth."

Georgia wasn't convinced. "Are you going to select who goes and who stays? I don't want that task. And instead of hope, it's only delaying the inevitable. There has to be another, better way."

Megan shook her head in disbelief. "You're prepared to let Redmayne and the Professor leave and condemn the rest of us to death. After what he's done? Georgia, you've become blinded by your desire to build a better society. Can't you see it's not ready for that? Maybe it never will be. You have to think straight and save our people. At least you'll be alive to try again. We've been beaten by Zhang. It's time to admit defeat and escape while we still can. Please!"

"Megan's right," said Jackson. "You've tried the best you can but we're out of options. Let the governments back on Earth deal with the matter. If they refuse to re-supply the general, then he and his crew will be starved off the planet. And we can return and start again."

The conversation ceased as Molloy, Anna and Mancuso entered the control room, looking dejected at their failure to repair the particle accelerator. Georgia walked across to Anna and shook her hand. "Welcome Professor. I wish we were meeting under different circumstances."

"Thank you, commander. I am sorry I could not be of any help. Did we interrupt your conversation?"

Georgia quickly repeated over the main points of her discussion with General Zhang, before outlining the options, or lack of them, that were available. "Is there any means of disrupting the particle beam, to reduce its effectiveness?" she asked, looking at Molloy and Anna for an answer.

Both shook their heads. Molloy said, "I thought about this on the journey back from *Yorktown*. If we fired the main engines on the remaining ships, we could create a large dust cloud that would hinder their targeting ability. The beam would still slice through the cloud, vaporizing the dust particles and destroying anything in its path. And we don't have enough fuel to do that more than once. You'd need to know when to expect the attack too so that the rockets could be started before the general is within range."

"We do know when the general will attack," exclaimed Jackson. "He told us we had four hours. That was nearly fifteen minutes ago but it allows us to plot his orbits and where he'll be attacking from. Surely, we can narrow that down even further with satellite analysis. Can't Ground Control help with that?"

"It's a defensive measure and still doesn't allow enough time to prepare *Lexington*, even if we prevent it from being a target first time around. It will still be there on the next opportunity Zhang has, and then he'll have a clear shot," said Georgia. The room went quiet as everyone accepted that the position looked bleak.

Redmayne had been sitting silently for several minutes, largely ignored by everyone else in the control room. He took the opportunity to say, "there is another way, but I'm not sure you're going to like it."

Chapter 28

Georgia sat down across from Redmayne. Despite the fact she was reluctant to listen to anything the man had to say, now was not the time to be constrained by the past. In any case, no one in the room had anything to suggest and they were running out of time. "Okay Redmayne, what's your solution?"

Redmayne waited a few seconds, for dramatic effect. It was clear he wanted everyone to pay full attention. "You're right about defense being useless against the Chinese. It only delays the inevitable. So, we must do something more proactive. You can thank Jackson for this suggestion. He's absolutely correct that we can plot the *Taipei*'s orbit thanks to Zhang's indiscretion. We would have needed that information to more precisely target your particle beam, if it was still functioning. However, we can still attack the general in other ways." He paused again and walked to the window, fully aware of the pairs of eyes follow him as he crossed the room. "With the spaceships at your disposal, you could use one effectively as a missile to stop him in his tracks. It's the last thing he'll be expecting."

Mancuso didn't like how smug Redmayne looked. "Great idea, Einstein. Unfortunately, none of the supply ships are fitted with sophisticated enough guidance to hit an object traveling at over fourteen thousand miles an hour. *Lexington* is the only vessel that could possible do what you suggest, but it's now loaded with half our supplies and is our only way off Mars. If we need to leave in the event of an emergency, we don't have any other human rated ships."

Georgia agreed, "You're right Joe. None of our ships make viable missiles. But Redmayne's on to something. And he has the Russian landing craft. Perhaps we could use that instead."

"No, wait," objected Anna. "*Kiev* is my escape route back to *Moskva*. You promised we would be allowed to leave if I came here to help you.

It was a huge disappointment that your weapon was irreparable, but I have done what you asked. Are you now breaking your promise?"

"I'm sorry, Professor," replied Georgia. "I wish there was another way. You must be able to see that I need options to save everyone here. Remember, it is your comrade that suggested this course of action after all."

Anna sneered at Redmayne. "He is no comrade of mine. He is a traitor and cannot be trusted. Perhaps no Americans can be trusted."

Megan laughed, "I guess you found it hard to make friends at Derzost too, Redmayne. Surely that should tell you something about your character."

"There's no time for cheap jibes," said Georgia. "I need to know if using *Kiev* as a missile is possible."

"Yes, it's possible," replied Redmayne, reluctantly. "It would require precise calculation as the closing speed of the two vehicles would be close to eighteen thousand miles an hour. That's five miles per second. And the target is maybe thirty feet wide."

"But we only get one shot at this. If you miss, then we're sitting targets," said Jackson. "With that level of precision, I don't fancy the odds of success."

"There's a sure way of improving those odds," said Molloy. "You're thinking of *Kiev* as one giant missile. If that was true than I'd rate the chances of success as slightly better than zero. However, if there's a way we can detonate *Kiev* a fraction of a second before it reaches Zhang's ship, we create millions of deadly projectiles covering a wider area. It only takes one or two of those projectiles to impact the target. At five miles per second, their ship will be obliterated. That is a far more realistic alternative."

"It certainly is," said Georgia, suddenly more positive. "Does anyone have anything to add?"

Anna said, "I still have objections to remaining here. None of you were at Derzost when it was attacked. You have no idea how terrifying the experience was, and I don't want to go through it again. But if this is the best opportunity of saving the crew, then I am willing to agree to the plan."

"Before we get ahead of ourselves, there is one major obstacle," added Redmayne. "Someone will need to pilot *Kiev*. Its computer systems are designed to take it to the Russian mother ship with the use of directional beacons. We don't have time to rewrite the navigational programs for automated flight. Someone will need to be aboard the vessel to take manual control and override the guidance systems. In fact, it will require two people; one to pilot the ship and the other to calculate any deviations to the trajectory. However accurately we plot the Chinese ship, we'll need to take account of course corrections and there will only be a few seconds to do so."

"So, it's a suicide mission!" exclaimed Jackson. "You want people to sacrifice themselves in order to save the rest of us."

Redmayne shook his head. "Not necessarily. *Kiev* does have an escape pod. But there is no denying the fact that whoever is on board will be risking their lives. I wouldn't like to calculate the odds of survival."

"I knew it was too good to be true," said Mancuso bitterly. "You have a way of being a huge disappointment."

Redmayne shrugged. "Georgia wanted options. I've given you a very good one. It may not be perfect and there are consequences. Do you have anything better to offer?"

Mancuso blushed and looked as if he wanted to punch Redmayne. Somehow, he managed to restrain any violent urges he had.

"You seem to have the most experience with that landing craft. Are you prepared to risk your life or are you expecting one of us to save your miserable existence?" asked Megan, keen to see Redmayne's reaction.

"Megan, if we proceed with this plan, we can't force anyone to carry it out," interrupted Georgia. "We need to stay calm."

"The Doctor's right though," said Redmayne. "It's my idea and I am the only one here with any experience of flying that vehicle. After what

I've done, I can't expect anyone to risk their life for me. I'll pilot *Kiev* if that's the plan you decide to go with."

Georgia nodded. "Okay, time for a vote then. Does everyone agree to taking out General Zhang with the Russian landing craft?" She looked around the room as everyone slowly showed their approval. "Thank you. In that case, there's no time to waste in making the necessary calculations. Jackson, I believe you have some explosives for your seismic sources, as well as some remote detonators. We'll need those in order to blow up the *Kiev*."

"Yes, I do, sis," he replied. "They're still on one of the supply ships but easily accessible. I know where they are."

"Joe, go with Jackson and retrieve what we need. Then report to me on *Kiev* so we can install the explosives in a suitable location."

"I'm on it, Georgia," Mancuso replied as he headed out of the door, followed closely by Jackson.

Molloy said, "there's still the question of who accompanies Redmayne. You need someone who can make spontaneous calculations under extreme pressure. There's no room for error in either targeting Zhang or using the escape pod at exactly the right time. Chances of success are extremely small"

Georgia stood up to face Molloy. "I'm fully aware of that, lieutenant. That's why I'm going to be his co-pilot!"

Chapter 29

Georgia hurried along the corridors to her quarters with Megan scampering close behind. "You can't do this Georgia. Order someone else to go in your place."

"Who should I send? Mancuso? Or how about Molloy? I can't order anyone to do it, Megan. It has to be me. I'm as competent as anyone else here to read the instrumentation and make any course alterations."

"It's no time for heroics. You're too important to this mission and to me."

"I have no intention of dying today or anytime soon. I've cheated death more than once and I can do it again." By now, Georgia had reached her quarters and was searching through a drawer for a change of clothes.

"You're not indestructible, Georgia! You've been lucky so far, but everyone's luck runs out eventually."

Pulling her t shirt over her head, Georgia replied, "My mind's made up. You know me well enough by now to know how stubborn I am."

"I do. But I wouldn't be your best friend if I didn't try to stop you."

Georgia sat down on the bed to change her trousers. She knew Megan meant well and provided sound advice. There had been days when she wondered how she could have coped without Megan's friendship. In fact, she was the only person other than Jackson that Georgia had ever relied on or trusted completely. She stood up and gave Megan a hug, holding her tight until she thought she might start crying. "I knew you understood. I promise you I'm coming back. I know I'm not invincible, but I have to do this for me, as well as everyone else on the base."

Megan wiped her eyes. "Don't let me down. I'm not ready to spend the next two years here without you. You're like having a little sister. We confide in each other. I'm never going to be able to have the same conversations with anyone else."

"Maybe not. But you need to get back to the medical center and start packing. You all need to be away from the base in case this plan doesn't work."

***

Redmayne was waiting for Georgia by the main airlock. Molloy had been told about his previous actions and was watching him closely, ensuring he behaved himself.

Redmayne smiled as Georgia approached. "I offer to put my life at risk for the base and you still don't trust me," he said.

She marched up to him, looking him squarely in the eyes. "I'll never trust you, whatever you say or do. What we're about to do is not an act of redemption. It's borne through necessity. Not for one moment does this wipe out the murders you committed. Remember, you're responsible for the deaths of some good men, with families. I'll be grateful if this plan works, but that is as far as it goes."

She turned and began to climb into her spacesuit, controlling her breathing to regain her calmness.

Redmayne stared at her, hardly recognizing the strong woman he saw in front of him. Was this what he had done to her? He didn't recall her being so assertive or full of anger. Two years earlier, she had been far easier to manipulate. Now, he saw a natural leader who understood her own mind and appeared to be respected by her crew. He could appreciate why people would follow her. If circumstances were different, he'd do the same. He glanced at Molloy and received another cold stare in return.

There was a spare spacesuit hanging up that looked approximately his size. He climbed into it, carefully checking the seals around the gloves and boots before pulling the helmet over his head and following Georgia into the airlock. After her recent outburst, he decided it was best not to try any more small talk. Georgia maintained her silence as they stepped out of the airlock and onto the hectic plain in front of Alpha Base.

The pair of them climbed onto a pair of nearby speeders and headed out in the direction of the Russian landing craft, passing several astronauts who were making their way to *Lexington* on foot. A robotic tractor was towing a trailer laden with supplies. The scene reminded Redmayne of wartime evacuations he'd only ever seen on television. To be part of an actual evacuation was surreal.

Georgia finally spoke as they approached the dark silhouette of *Kiev*. "You head inside and commence the pre-launch checklist. I need to check on progress at *Lexington*. And don't think of leaving without me." Georgia altered her course without another word, leaving Redmayne to stare after her.

***

Around the base of *Lexington* was a hive of activity. Georgia spotted Vicky Morris in the middle of all the organized chaos, coordinating the loading of supplies onto the huge spaceship, and the stacking of pallets arriving from the supply ships. There was a steady train of robotic tractors and trailers traveling to and fro between ships, with astronauts shepherding supplies. It looked chaotic but Georgia appreciated it was all being well controlled efficiently by Vicky. At any other time, it would be a joy to behold.

She slowly rolled up to where Vicky was standing, careful not to get in the way of a robotic trailer carrying two large white pallets. "How's it going?" she asked, already knowing the answer.

Vicky had seen Georgia's approach and was expecting the question. "Okay so far, commander. There have been no equipment failures which means we're ahead of schedule. I'm concerned that we have less than an hour of daylight left. The darkness will slow us down and the temperature drop will cause problems with the tractor units. We can use their heaters but that will drain the batteries. However, we will be finished long before all the fuel has been pumped in."

"Excellent work, Vicky. Don't tell Joe but you're easily as good as him." Georgia gave her a friendly wink. "We have a plan which means we hopefully won't need to use *Lexington* to abandon the planet. However, it's reassuring to know that the ship will be ready if my plan doesn't work out."

"Good luck," replied Vicky. "I'm sure you'll succeed. I believe in you."

***

Georgia found her way from the airlock to the command deck where Redmayne was busy working through complex calculations on one of the computers. The interior of *Kiev* was far more basic than Georgia had expected. The corridor from the airlock was dark and claustrophobic, with a metallic floor that echoed with every step she took. Bare gray walls were streaked with dents and scrapes from numerous cosmonauts passing back and forth. The flight deck was sparse and dimly lit, with most of the light coming from the two computer monitors. For Georgia, the whole ambiance felt quite depressing after the open spaces and brightness of Alpha Base. *No wonder the Russians are always so miserable*, she thought.

"How are your calculations progressing?" she asked when Redmayne failed to acknowledge she'd walked in. Or maybe he was just ignoring her.

He stopped what he was doing and sat back in his seat. "Frustratingly slowly. There are too many variables at the moment. We only need to be a degree out or get the speed wrong and we'll miss the target completely. This is far more complex than I expected."

"I understand that, but is it possible? If not, then we desperately need a new plan." Redmayne's statement made her nervous to have trusted him on this, there final hope of survival.

"I didn't say I couldn't do it," he replied. "Any additional information we can get on Zhang's position will be an immense benefit. Don't worry Georgia, I think this is still our best plan."

"You'd better be right about this. Everyone else is expecting you to fail. General Stockton has targeted Zhang with all the satellites we have in Martian orbit. They should shortly give us a detailed picture of his orbital trajectory and inclination. Unless Zhang performs any late course corrections, the *Taipei* will be in the exact place we expect it to be."

"Thanks for letting me know. I've been literally pulling my hair out for the past ten minutes. I need that information soon or there won't be time to complete the calculations."

"They'll be through within the next fifteen minutes. Are you sure this ship will get us there?"

Redmayne laughed. "Don't be fooled by the aesthetics. I know how *Kiev* looks but the Russians know how to make reliable spacecraft. She'll work fine and do the job when we need her to."

Georgia wasn't convinced but it was too late to find an alternate plan. This had to work although the bravado she'd felt speaking with Megan was beginning to sound hollow.

"We have visitors," Redmayne said as a red light on the console in front of him began to flash. "That will be Mancuso and your brother."

Another battle to face, thought Georgia. If Megan had been hard to convince, telling Jackson that she was going to risk her life would be almost impossible. She wanted to talk to him in private. "Redmayne, while we're waiting for the data, you can go help Mancuso plant the explosives. You know the best places to locate them for maximum impact. It won't be the first time you've blown something up." Georgia knew it was a low blow, but she couldn't help herself. *He deserves it.*

Redmayne looked as if he was about to reply, but instead he quickly headed toward the airlock. A minute later, a disturbed looking Jackson stepped into the room. "What's happening sis? Why are you here?"

"Take a seat, Jacko," she replied. "I'm going with Redmayne. He needs someone to monitor *Taipei*'s course and make any minor adjustments before we detonate the explosives. I'm the best person to do that."

"Bullshit!" exclaimed Jackson as he jumped back to his feet. "What about Joe? He's a pilot. So is Major Stoddard. They can easily go in your place. There's no need to risk your own life."

"And who's going to pilot *Lexington* if this fails or I'm killed? Joe and Stoddard are too valuable to the remaining twenty crewmen and women. I'm the most logical choice. But I'll be back to kick your ass." She smiled weakly, unable to fool herself this time. Jackson made her appreciate how much she could lose. This had to be the craziest and riskiest plan she'd ever taken part in. The stakes were phenomenally high, and doubt was starting to creep into her thoughts. But the last thing she needed now was for her fears to betray her to her younger brother.

Jackson stared at her, open mouthed. "No doubt you've fooled Megan into thinking this mission is safe enough, but I can tell when you're scared. You know there's a good chance you'll not make it."

Georgia nodded slowly. "Yes, there's always that possibility. But I've taken risks before and they're paid off. It's worth taking one more risk to save the personnel on the base."

"You don't even know most of them yet. They've only been here two days."

"That doesn't matter. I want to get to know them. If they've been selected for the Mars program, then I'm sure they're all good men and women who deserve a chance to survive. And to experience the wonders this planet has to offer."

"By sacrificing your life?"

"If necessary. Although I hope it doesn't come to that." Georgia heard her voice waver and cursed herself for revealing her nerves.

"You've always taken care of me, sis. It's about time I returned the favor. Let me go in your place. I can do this."

Jackson's plea tugged at her heartstrings. She loved her brother so much and looking after him was as natural to her as breathing. "No, you can't. Not this time. Thanks for the offer, Jacko. It really does have to be me. I'm sorry but that's the way is has to be. I will do all I can to get back to you though. I don't think I've ever let you down yet." She leaned forward and, like she had with Megan, hugged him close to her. This time, she was unable to hold back the tears that ran down her face and she felt Jackson sobbing in her arms.

They were still like that when Redmayne and Mancuso entered the room several minutes later. "What's going on here?" asked Mancuso, feeling embarrassed at interrupting a private family moment.

Georgia reluctantly broke the embrace with her brother and said, "Joe, I need you to take Jackson with you. I'm going with Redmayne to destroy Zhang's ship. I'm putting you in charge until I return. Which should be in the next hour or so."

Mancuso was stunned by the news. He looked at Georgia as if she'd spoke a foreign language, before turning to Redmayne and then at Jackson as the words finally sank in. He reached out to Jackson. "Come on, we have to go. I'm sure Georgia knows what she's doing."

Jackson was trying hard to recover his composure. He wasn't ready to let his sister go but recognized that he was outnumbered. He gave Georgia one final hug before leading Mancuso back toward the airlock.

"Are you okay?" Redmayne asked once they had gone.

"It's no business of yours," she snapped. In reality she wanted to throw up. Saying goodbye to her brother was the hardest thing she had done. She hoped the pain was worth it.

Chapter 30

Georgia tightened the straps on her seat until she was unable to move. Satisfied that she was as secure as she needed to be, she returned her attention to the rows of numbers on the computer screen in front of her. In the top right hand corner, the countdown clock showed there were only four minutes until take-off. After a momentary panic thinking about the enormity of the challenge ahead, she took a deep breath and focused entirely on what was happening inside the control room. There was no longer time to be worried about external distractions. She was focused solely on successfully achieving this mission.

"How are the pre-launch checks progressing?" she asked without looking up from her own screen.

"Still no anomalies. The flight computers are in self alignment and the primary fuel tanks are up to flight pressure. Hydraulic systems are green, and the igniter purge is complete. In two minutes we'll be going for final engine cooldown."

It was what she needed to hear. There couldn't be delays of any kind at this stage.

She flicked the comms button to contact Alpha Base. "Joe, has everyone pulled back from *Lexington*?"

"That's confirmed. They're a safe distance away for your take-off and will stay so until the threat has passed. I'm here with Megan. We're the only ones left on the base. Everyone else has evacuated."

"You need to leave too Joe, as soon as we've taken off. You won't be safe there if we fail."

"That's a negative, Georgia. Someone has to monitor your progress. And I'm not expecting you to fail. You've got this. And in case you don't, we're both wearing our spacesuits. They may give us half a chance."

Georgia had no time to argue and in fact felt reassured by Mancuso's message.

"You're a pain in the ass, Joe. But I wouldn't have it any other way. Pray this works. Georgia out."

"Two minutes to launch," Redmayne called unnecessarily. "Thrust vector actuator test complete. Flight computer to start-up."

Georgia lowered the visor on her helmet and snapped it in place. She remembered how much she hated take-off. It was the same fear she felt on roller coasters on the slow climb to the top before the adrenaline rush of the sudden vertical drop. This was different though. She was in a dilapidated Russian vessel that looked as if it belonged in a museum, and the stakes were so much higher.

"This is going to work isn't it?" she asked Redmayne one more time.

"If you're worried about *Kiev*, looks can be deceiving. The ship may look like it belongs in a museum, but it's been a reliable workhorse. It's also the only shot we've got. I would give us a sixty-five percent chance of success but ask me again in seven minutes."

With thirty seconds left to go until launch, the knot in her stomach was almost unbearable. So many things could still go wrong. So many people were relying on her to succeed. She took one long, slow deep breath and remembered why she was doing this and the many things that had gone right. The people who now called Alpha Base their home deserved an opportunity to experience mars in all its glory. She deserved more time to spend with her brother. The pain in in stomach diminished as she thought more about what she had to gain from defeating the Chinese general.

She opened her eyes again and watched mesmerized as the clock counted down the final ten seconds. At the one second mark, she heard a distant roar as the powerful rocket engines fired up. The next moment, she was being pushed back violently into her seat as *Kiev* soared into the sky, accelerating hard. Everything in the flight deck was shaking and rattling so much it was almost impossible to read the data on the screen in front of her. The sound was deafening. Far worse than anything she'd experienced on *Endeavour* during landing. It was no small miracle how the ship was holding together.

Thirty-five seconds after launch, Redmayne throttled back the engines to ninety five percent causing the vibrations and the noise to subside. "How are we tracking?" she shouted so that Redmayne could hear her.

"We're on the mark at the moment. Four minutes to target. Any updates on Zhang's position?"

"The screen's not refreshed any numbers. We should be receiving the final coordinates within the next few seconds." Georgia crossed her fingers. If *Taipei* had adjusted its orbit in the last thirty minutes, it would be too late to make any material course correction.

She frowned as she saw the numbers on her screen alter. After scanning the lines of data, she called out, "no change to direction but their altitude is five hundred feet higher than the previous reading and their speed has reduced by eight hundred miles per hour. They're giving themselves more of a window to target Alpha Base. I've sent you the new vector. Can you make the necessary adjustments?"

Redmayne could be seen quickly typing information into his computer. "Course correction is being plotted in now. Their reduced velocity allows us another two seconds, which could make all the difference. If the information is correct, there's six hundred and twenty miles between us. So only two minutes to see if this plan of mine was a fool's errand."

***

On board *Taipei*, the air of eager anticipation had returned. The past few orbits had tested their patience but that was now completely forgotten.

"Three minutes until we are in range of the American base, General," reported Colonel Liu calmly.

Zhang and Liu had spent the past hour considering which should be the primary target. Although Alpha Base was the obvious choice, Zhang's conversation with the base's commander had made the general wonder whether the *Lexington* should be his primary focus after all. Liu had explained that it made more sense to destroy the American's only means of escape before returning to complete the destruction of the base itself. The complete loss of personnel as well as the base would have a profound effect on America and provide an undeniable demonstration of his weapon's power. If the weak politicians in his government wanted to negotiate, they would be doing so from a position of absolute power. Now was the time to be decisive.

Coughing to clear his throat, he ordered, "Huang, target their crew ship first. I want the Americans trapped. If they're preparing *Lexington* for escape, it will be easy for you to spot on the infrared scanner."

Major Huang had been expecting to target the base and was surprised by the general's late change of heart. But she knew better than to question the general's orders. "As you wish, sir. I'll target their fuel tanks. It won't be difficult for the particle beam to rupture the skin of their vehicle. If they are refueling then the effect will be spectacular. The explosion will light up the area for miles around"

"Make sure you record everything," reminded Liu. "This will make excellent propaganda. General, am I correct in thinking the base is now the secondary target? We may have time to attack that as well on this pass if we don't expend too much energy on their ship."

"Of course, Colonel. Let's show the Earth the devastation we can rain down on our enemies."

***

Georgia remained focused on her own monitor for any final alterations. Time had slowed as her mind went through hundreds of permutations and searched for any discrepancies in the information being presented to her. Redmayne's voice cut into her thoughts.

"Georgia, the escape pod is primed. Once we seal the hatch, I've programmed a five second countdown. The explosive detonators are on a two second timer which should be enough for the pod to escape the blast radius. I suggest you make your way to the pod now. There's nothing more you can do here."

Georgia unbuckled her restraints and tried to move. Because *Kiev* was still accelerating, it was harder than she had anticipated to move, and she was grateful she had not delayed the decision. Pulling herself slowly forward, she was acutely aware of the time it was taking. As she reached the pod's hatch there was only forty seconds until impact and Redmayne was still at his controls.

"Come on Redmayne. It's time to go," she called to him. As she did so, she lost her grip and slid rapidly along the floor toward the rear of the flight deck. She gasped in pain as she hit the wall hard, her leg twisting awkwardly beneath her. She struggled to find her balance as she stood back up, frantic that she wouldn't be able to make it to the pod in time. Fighting off the panic that was setting in, she felt Redmayne grasp her wrist tightly and pull her roughly back to the pod. She found herself being roughly pushed inside the small escape vehicle which was more basic than the rest of the ship. There was one computer screen, two seats and a small round viewing window. Georgia climbed into one of the seats and began fumbling for the restraints. Redmayne quickly followed her into the pod, sealed the hatch and sat opposite her, holding the remote detonator.

"Five seconds!" he exclaimed as she tried and failed to attach the restraint at the front of her. Her hands couldn't grasp the buckle and her right knee was screaming in agony. All too soon, she saw Redmayne press the trigger on the detonator as a fraction of a second later, the pod's rockets fired, and they accelerated away from *Kiev* at eight g's. Georgia was forcibly thrown from her seat, slamming hard into the bulkhead next to the hatch before passing out.

***

Major Huang was the first to see the unexpected reading on her main computer screen. "General, I'm picking up a heat signature in the upper atmosphere. A vehicle appears to have launched from Alpha Base."

"But that's impossible!" exclaimed Zhang. "Liu, you said the Americans didn't have time to fuel their ship in time. You've let them escape. I told you we should have changed our orbit."

"It's too small to be *Lexington*. And it's on a strange trajectory."

"Let me take a look," said Liu, leaning across to look at the blurred image on Huang's scanner. Using the controls to zoom in and sharpen the focus he identified the object. "It's a Russian landing craft," he said in surprise. "They must be ferrying some of their crew to *Moskva*."

Zhang was furious they had allowed anyone to escape, but immediately decided against shooting down the craft. His priority had to be the American base. "It seems we weren't as efficient at destroying Derzost as we thought," he said. "No matter, we can round these escapees up later. They've only delayed the inevitable. Continue with the mission as planned and no more fuck ups. I want *Lexington* and the base obliterated from the face of the planet"

"Yes general," replied Liu, relieved that the general hadn't taken out his fury on him. "Thirty seconds until target acquisition. Power is at one hundred percent and cooling of the particle accelerator is complete. I have programmed a twenty-five second burst for their spaceship. Countdown commencing in ten seconds."

Colonel Liu was interrupted by Huang's frantic shout. "The Russian craft is heading straight for us!" There was no mistaking the terror in her voice. "They're going to hit us!"

"Take evasive action!" ordered Zhang. How did the Americans know where we would be?

Reactively, Huang fired the forward rocker motors at maximum thrust to reduce *Taipei*'s altitude, hoping the maneuver would be enough to move them out of the way. The oncoming ship was now a shining dot on the main view screen and was only a matter of seconds away. "This will be close," she said, knowing that it would take a moment for *Taipei* to react to the course correction.

"Good work, Huang," said Zhang, humiliated he had been outsmarted by his enemy on this occasion. The attack would have to wait but the ultimate victory would taste sweeter. He would enjoy making them pay for their insolence.

But as Zhan watched the screen and cursed his luck, a number of actions caught his eye. A small rocket quickly shot away from the side of the oncoming Russian ship. And then, to his horror, the Russian ship explode in a ball of flames and continued to head in his direction. He glanced in disbelief at Liu who stared back despairingly.

Zhang braced himself for the inevitable impact, shouting defiantly at the screen. One second later, *Taipei* was shredded as it sped through *Kiev's* debris field. An instant later, a huge fireball briefly lit the night sky as *Taipei's* propellant exploded. Millions of metal fragments glowed bright orange as they rained down on Mars, with several larger pieces tumbling end over end, the final evidence that *Taipei* had ever existed.

Chapter 31

The escape pod's rocket motors, their job done, quickly died as the fuel was expended. The acceleration ended but the pod was now tumbling end over end. Georgia came around, being gently shaken by a concerned looking Redmayne. She felt bruised and physically sick. Her knee was still throbbing and felt like she'd sprained her ligaments. But at least she was alive.

"How long was I out?" she asked.

"Ten seconds, max," he replied. "I think the flight computer has malfunctioned. Retro rockets should have stabilized the pod by now. We're out of control."

"Did we succeed in stopping the Chinese?"

"I think so. I saw *Kiev* explode and I doubt Zhang had time to react."

"I hope you're right. But I guess we now have something else to worry about."

Georgia was becoming disoriented by the spinning pod. A small porthole showed Mars spinning by. There was no way to tell which direction they were traveling in and they could easily be heading out into space.

Georgia found the computer interface and keyed in a few commands. The screen remained blank. *Great! Now what am I supposed to do?* Out of frustration she hit the corner of the screen hard with the palm of her hand and was surprised to be rewarded with the screen flickering to life. Unfortunately, she was faced with a screen full of meaningless Cyrillic symbols. "I need your help here. Someone forgot to upgrade the pod's computer system."

Redmayne leaned over and pressed a button that transitioned the symbols into the western alphabet.

"Thanks," she said as she attempted to kick start the guidance system. At the third attempt, the screen showed the data she was looking for. "The good news is we're returning to Mars," she said as she read through the information. "We're currently at an altitude of ninety-six miles and falling rapidly."

"I there any way you can prevent us from crashing into the ground?" Redmayne asked sardonically.

"I'm doing my best." Georgia keyed in some random commands, before shouting, "Eureka!" She pressed a button on the keyboard and felt a series of thrusters firing. Within seconds, the tumbling slowed and then stopped. Mars was now sixty-eight miles below them and filled the view from the porthole. There was no time to congratulate herself as they were still traveling at three thousand miles an hour.

"Get strapped back in. I'm firing the retro rockets in five seconds," she warned. This time she made sure she was secured in her seat before firing the rockets. The pod instantly began to decelerate, forcing both Georgia and Redmayne deep into their seats. Georgia gasped as she struggled to breathe. She could only manage short shallow breaths, each one painful. Her main concern was whether the retro rockets had sufficient fuel as they continued to hurtle toward the ground.

Forty seconds later, the roar of the rocket motors died. Georgia checked the computer screen and saw they were now only eight miles high with a velocity of two hundred miles per hour. Time for the computer to deploy the parachutes. But something was wrong. There was no sensation of drag. In fact, they were in free fall again and plummeting toward the ground.

***

Molloy and Jackson were walking slowly back toward *Lexington* with the rest of the crew, scanning the night sky for some kind of sign. Twenty seconds earlier, they'd seen two brief flashes just above the distant horizon, the second brighter than the first, but still had no idea whether Georgia had been successful. "What do you think?" asked Jackson. The waiting was unbearable.

"We'll know in the next two minutes," replied Molloy. "If we don't see the particle beam in that time then it's a fairly safe bet that the Chinese vessel has been destroyed or at least damaged. It looks as if there was at least one explosion and probably two. That's a positive sign."

"But is Georgia safe?"

"That will take longer to discover. You'll need to check with Mancuso to see if there's been any communication. One step at a time. Let's pray your sister succeeded and we survive."

"I shouldn't have let her go. If she's died saving my life, then I'm never going to forgive myself. She's the only family I have."

"Jackson, from what I've seen and heard about Georgia there is no way she would have let you go in her place. She knows what she's doing and is the best person to make the plan work." Molloy paused to look at the other astronauts standing around him, staring up at the heavens. "Everyone here knows what's at stake and has confidence in Georgia."

Jackson stood in silence, counting down the seconds and waiting for a beam of light to suddenly appear from a point in the sky. As the two-minute mark approached, he held his breath in the hope that there would be no last-minute attack. One minute later and Mancuso's voice could be heard by everyone when he said, "All clear. It looks as if Commander Pyke succeeded."

A universal cheer could be heard across the comms channel as relief swept through everyone standing around *Lexington* in the darkness.

"What now?" asked Jackson, allowing a mixture of emotions to wash over him.

"Go back to Alpha and wait to hear from Georgia or Redmayne," replied Molloy. "I'm sure they'll be communicating their location anytime soon."

Jackson quickly located a speeder close by and headed for the distant lights of Alpha Base, still fearful of Georgia's fate.

***

"Override the firing mechanism for the parachute bolts!" screamed Redmayne.

"What do you think I'm trying to do?" exclaimed Georgia, remaining calm as her brain calculated the options available to her in the few seconds available before their velocity would be too great for the parachutes to work. There was nothing of obvious help on the computer screen. There had to be another way. Looking around the sparse and cramped interior of the escape pod, she noticed a large red handle with large red Cyrillic writing next to the hatch. "Above your head! Pull that handle."

Redmayne reached up and pulled down on the handle as hard as he could. It moved about four inches before he could pull it no further. Nothing happened for maybe half a second and then the pod seemed to hit something as its descent was slowed. Georgia and Redmayne were forced hard into their seats with the force.

"That will be the drogue chute," Redmayne said, the relief obvious in his voice. In a few seconds it should pull out the main chutes. Sure enough, the pod lurched as the huge main parachutes flared and bellowed before beginning to slow the rate of descent.

Georgia could feel a slow swaying motion as the pod hung below the two enormous parachutes. It was a strange sensation that made her feel queasy. Looking through the porthole, all she could see was blackness. Wherever they were above Mars, it was still night and there was no visual way of seeing where they were or what the landscape below held for them. They could be above a mountain or a deep gorge and they would have no idea.

The data on the computer screen showed their rate of descent was continuing to slow but remained more than eighty miles per hour. If they hit the ground at that speed it would be the equivalent of a fly hitting a windshield.

"I don't suppose you were trained on the escape pod to know how we can slow our vertical velocity?" she asked Redmayne who now appeared to have recovered his composure.

"No, I was only shown the basics to fly between Derzost and the orbiting Andropov. There was no one to show me the in-flight safety procedures. I would imagine the landing is automated with the retro rockets firing at a specified height above the ground. That's just my guess though."

"So, we just wait and hope?" Georgia regretted not asking sooner, although the answer would not have altered the plan. "What about an emergency beacon? We need to inform Mancuso so he can mount a rescue mission."

"Again, it should be part of the automated system. Unless you can see anything on the computer screen."

"Ah, yes," she muttered as she pressed a button in the top left corner. "I know Jackson and some of the crew will be worried about us."

"They'll be concerned for your safety," corrected Redmayne, bitterly. "No one's going to be thinking about me."

Georgia could sense the escape pod spinning as well as swaying. She was not enjoying the experience and was convinced the movement was going to make her throw up any time soon. "What do you expect?" she said, trying to ignore her nausea. "Redmayne, you did a fantastic job saving Alpha and rescuing me. I am truly grateful for that. But I can never stop despising you for what you did."

"That's understandable. I hate myself most days so I can't expect forgiveness from you or anyone else. I didn't do this to make amends for my crimes. I know I have to face the consequences for those deaths and I'm ready to be held accountable. I've been living a lie for the last two years, fooling myself that I could escape justice."

Georgia looked at him in the dim interior light of the pod. *Perhaps he's changed after all, but he can't alter what he's done*, she thought. "I'll need to decide what to do with you. *Lexington* isn't due to return to Earth for another twenty months and I don't know what effect your presence will have on the rest of the crew. To be honest, I don't even know what jurisdiction you'd be tried under. We're breaking new ground here."

At that moment, and without warning, the retro rockets briefly fired for a fraction of a second, causing the escape pod to violently slow. Georgia had a moment to glance at the rate of descent and note that it was still too fast. Before she could brace herself, the pod careened into the ground at an angle and skidded across a rock outcrop. Badly winded by the crash landing, she heard the tortured screeching of metal as it was forcefully torn from the underside of the escape pod. The computer screen went immediately blank and the emergency light failed, leaving her in complete darkness, as the pod continued to bump and slide along the ground before coming to a halt.

Georgia found herself laid on her side but still strapped into her seat. She gasped, trying to recover her breathing as pain threatened to engulf her. Her right knee was still in agony but now her lower back felt bruised as well as both shoulders where the straps had cut into her. At least her spacesuit was in one piece, maintaining the integrity of her air supply.

"Redmayne, are you okay?" she called out into the darkness. There was no reply. After loosening her straps, she felt around in the dark for the flashlight she could remember seeing earlier. She found it and was relieved that it was working. Moving carefully because of her injuries she shone the light toward where Redmayne had been sitting. Instead of finding him in his seat, she was appalled to see that part of the pod had been ripped away in the crash, leaving an ugly hole, about five feet long.

Chapter 32

"How soon until we can mount a rescue mission," asked Jackson excitedly as he burst into Alpha's control room.

Mancuso, along with *Lexington*'s pilot, was busy checking the computer for a detailed topographical map of the area where the escape pod's emergency beacon had been detected. "It looks as though the escape pod came down about seven hundred and fifty miles west of here, in Kaiser Crater. I can fly *Lexington* sub-orbitally once we've loaded sufficient fuel for a return trip. I'm being told that will take another hour. I know that sounds like a long time, but I need to plot the course and find a suitable location to land. Remember, we've not surveyed that area of Mars in detail and I have to be sure we land on solid ground that will take the weight of the spaceship. I'm reluctant to land in the dark but I don't think we have the time to wait. The ultimate decision lies with Ground Control."

"I understand you're doing all that you can, Joe. Can I join you? I need to know that my sister is safe."

Mancuso had been expecting the question. "Yes, of course. There will be room for you alongside Doctor Betts, Lieutenant Molloy and Chief Engineer Qadir. If you want to keep busy in the meantime, find Vicky Morris back at *Lexington*. I've asked her to unload as much equipment and supplies to lighten the and make our trip easier. I'm sure she'll appreciate your assistance in moving the pallets clear of the launch area. I'll join you there in thirty minutes to prepare *Lexington* for launch."

Megan entered the control room as Jackson was leaving. "Has there been any radio communication, Joe?" she asked.

"Nothing yet," replied Mancuso. "They're out of range for their personal comms systems to work. If the escape pod has its own system, they've not used it."

"So we don't know if they survived."

"Georgia's alive," Mancuso replied defiantly. " Once we return her safely, we'll celebrate her success properly. Is your medical equipment ready? Just in case."

"It was already packed on *Lexington* in the event we had to leave. I've left Doctor Coleman to prepare the theater in case of surgery. We can't be too careful, and it makes him feel useful, which is apparently all he wants to be."

"Good thinking, Megan. Meet me at the airlock in twenty minutes." Mancuso returned to studying the map, scanning for any suitable landing spot.

***

Georgia crawled slowly through the hole in the side of the pod, careful not to snag her spacesuit on any of the jagged metal around the edge. Once safely through, she winced in pain as she stood up. Her knee felt as if someone was stabbing it with hot needles. Cautiously, she put more weight on her knee but knew she wouldn't be able to walk very far. Every other joint and muscle throbbed from the force of the landing, causing her to groan as she took a small step away from the escape pod and shone the light at it to see the extent of the damage.

She was surprised it had remained this intact. The force of the pod impacting the ground had been so severe she had expected the pod to have been destroyed. There were clear signs of metal being crumpled and badly dented by the crash, but the safety core had definitely done its job. Other than keep Redmayne safe!

She pointed the flashlight along the shallow gouge that the pod had created. Shards of metal glinted in the darkness as they reflected the light. Small rocks had been crushed or split as the pod had finished its final journey speeding across the Martian surface. There was no sign of Redmayne though. The eerie darkness enveloped everything that wasn't in the flashlight's beam, threatening to overwhelm her senses.

Dragging her right leg behind her, Georgia limped forward. Redmayne couldn't be far away. After about fifty yards, she spotted a large black object ahead of her. As she approached, she could see the object was the exterior section of the pod with one of Redmayne's legs sticking out from underneath. "Can you hear me," she called out expectantly, but there was only silence.

She grabbed an edge of the wreckage and pulled to see if she would be able to flip it over. It was immediately clear that it was too heavy for her to move on her own. She knelt down and peered underneath the twisted piece of metal to check on Redmayne's condition. Pointing her flashlight into the darkness she could see he was still strapped to his seat, laying face down with his helmet hanging several inches off the ground. She moved the light around, searching for any obvious sign of damage to his suit. There were no obvious telltale jets of vapor that would indicate a leak. But there was no way she could release his straps and remove him from the wreckage. She was going to have to wait for help to arrive and hope that her own suit didn't run out of power and air before then. Her heads-up display showed she was good for another three hours before there would there would be no power for her suit's heater. After that, it wouldn't take long for her to freeze to death.

***

On *Lexington*'s flight deck, Mancuso was systematically going through the pre-launch checklist with the ship's pilot, Major Stoddard, when he received the message from General Stockton he'd been waiting for. "We've reviewed your proposed flight profile and confirm that you are approved to proceed," said Stockton. "We understand that there is risk associated with the search and rescue mission, but it would be remiss of all of us if we didn't allow permission for you to save Commander Pyke. Not for the first time, she has put her own safety ahead of everyone else's. However, if you determine that a landing would endanger the *Lexington*, I trust that you will exercise sound judgment.

"I wanted to also let you know that interim feedback from our contacts in China is that *Taipei* was totally destroyed, with the death of General Zhang and two of his officers. This news has yet to be formally verified but our own satellites have been unable to detect *Taipei* in its expected orbit. So, I am confident that Alpha Base and its crew are now safe from any potential attacks.

"Give my congratulations to Georgia when you find her. As for Redmayne, put him in custody while we decide what to do with him. I have my own views on how he should be dealt with but, unfortunately, I don't have the authority. Have a safe and productive trip, Joe. Stockton out."

Mancuso smiled at the confidence being shown in him by the general. Now the pressure was on to find Georgia. He turned to Stoddard and said, "you heard the general. Let's get this show on the road."

***

Georgia was resting on the ground, conserving as much energy as possible. The flashlight was close by her side but switched off, leaving her in complete darkness. Her eyes had become accustomed to the lack of light and could make out indistinct shapes in the surrounding terrain which she guessed were either boulders or the rim of a small crater. Overhead, she could clearly see the Milky Way and the constellation of Orion. The unmistakable brightness of Betelgeuse and Rigel glimmered in the inky blackness, separated by the three stars of Orion's Belt.

In the silence and the darkness, Georgia was at one with the Universe. Although the base was hundreds of miles away and Redmayne was unconscious or dead, she had never felt less alone in her life. *If this is my time to die then I couldn't have chosen a better view*, she thought as she stared in awe at the stars. Despite the pain throughout her body, she had fallen into a light sleep several times, only to wake herself up when her head nodded forward.

"Where am I?" Redmayne's voice was weak and raspy.

"So, you are alive! I was starting to think the worst. You're lying under a fragment of the escape pod that was ripped off when we crash landed."

"That explains the darkness. How long ago was that?"

Georgia switched on the flashlight to check her chronometer. "About ninety minutes ago. You've not missed much since then. How are you feeling?"

"In agony! I think my legs are broken and I've cracked several ribs. Any idea when help is going to arrive?"

"There's been no contact with Alpha Base so far. I have no clue where we are. Because of our velocity at the time we ejected from *Kiev* we could be up to one thousand miles from the base. Joe Mancuso will be using *Lexington* to save us, but he would require some time to prepare the ship. Of course, if we failed then they could be dead and there's no one to rescue us anyway."

"Glad to hear you're so positive," coughed Redmayne. "Did you not think to get me down from here? These straps are digging into my shoulders and waist."

Georgia lowered herself to be able to look at Redmayne, shining the flashlight at him. "Your body weight prevented me from releasing you buckle. And my body is pretty banged up from the crash too. Thanks for asking!"

Redmayne grunted as he tried unsuccessfully to unclasp the buckle holding him in place. "It looks like I'll be staying here a while longer," he said, admitting defeat.

He coughed again and Georgia could see spots of blood on the inside of his helmet. "Try to relax and save your energy. I'm sure the rescue party will be here soon. All they have to do is follow the emergency beacon. I'm sure they'll be here soon."

Redmayne had also seen his blood though. "I don't think they'll be in time to save me," he said quietly, before making a strange gurgling sound.

"Don't talk like that. We still have hope. Doctor Betts will be part of the rescue team and she will be able to treat you. Just hold on."

There was no reply from Redmayne and his eyes were closed. She reached underneath the wreckage, shook him hard and was rewarded with his eyes flickering open.

"Stay with me, Tom. It's not your time to die. Concentrate on my voice and stay awake."

Redmayne managed a feeble smile. "I know you're doing your best, Georgia. But maybe it's better this way. I've got no future anywhere. At least my final act would be a positive one." He coughed again and this time there was much more blood.

"I never had you as a quitter. I thought you were a fighter. Like me. We're at our best when we're facing insurmountable odds."

There was a long pause before Redmayne responded. "We're not alike. You're a good person and deserve to survive." He stopped to catch his breath before continuing. "I've done terrible things which I hate myself for. You have no idea how hard it is living every day with my memories. If you only listen to one piece of advice from me, it is this. Do not stray from the person you are. If you behave with wicked intent it will slowly catch up with you and it will kill you."

"You made evil mistakes, Tom. But surely you can overcome those. Why give up now?"

There was a further bout of coughing and Tom's voice was now noticeably weaker as he replied, "There's no point trying to fool either of us. Society doesn't want people like me. And I don't blame them. I'm not looking for your pity. But I've had enough of being who I've turned into. I don't want to be saved anymore." Another coughing fit racked Redmayne's body before he slumped into unconsciousness.

Georgia shook him again but there was no response this time. She sat back up, leaning against the edge of the wreckage, confounded and annoyed at the tears rolling down her face.

Chapter 33

"Fifteen miles to target landing zone," Mancuso calmly called out, trying to ignore how strange it felt sitting in the captain's chair. *Lexington*'s pilot, Major Jack Stoddard, responded by applying some minor adjustments on the controls and checking the ship's trajectory.

Mancuso's instruments were showing a three-dimensional image of the terrain below them and he could see the *Lexington* was just passing over the eastern rim of the Kaiser Crater. At the edge of the image, a pulsing red light indicated the position of the escape pod's beacon, now less than ten miles away. The preferred landing zone was five hundred yards from the pod's location. That was the closest they dared land without fear of the landing rockets injuring Georgia or Redmayne with flying debris.

Out of a sense of hope more than expectation he tried to contact the downed astronauts. "Georgia? Redmayne? This is Mancuso on board *Lexington*. Can you hear me?" Unsurprisingly, there was nothing but static.

"Does that mean we're too late?" asked Jackson, a hint of desperation in his voice.

"Not at all," replied Mancuso. "There are plenty of possibilities why they're not responding. They must simply be preserving their power packs."

"Ten seconds before retro-firing," said Major Stoddard. If he was nervous at piloting his first sub-orbital flight, he wasn't showing it. Mancuso was pleased by the man's skills under extreme pressure.

Mancuso could now see an infrared image of the proposed landing zone. He adjusted the magnification to get a closer look for any large rocks or other impediments that could damage the ship but was satisfied with what he saw. "You're a go for landing, major."

"Roger that, sir."

One hundred and fifty feet beneath the flight deck, five of the huge rocket engines exploded into life, hurtling towers of flame toward the ground as they slowed *Lexington*'s velocity to almost zero. The extreme power of the engines could be felt through the astronauts' seats like a distant rumble of thunder. And then all was quiet again as the ship bumped gently onto the surface.

"Fantastic job, Jack," said Mancuso as he deftly unclipped his restraints and began the climb down to the cargo bay. "Can you make sure we're ready to return to Alpha Base as soon as we've recovered Georgia and Redmayne."

***

Georgia was sleeping again when she was taken by surprise as the black sky suddenly erupted in the blinding light from *Lexington*'s rockets. The light was so bright she had to shield her eyes with her hand as she watched *Lexington* descend and land on the far side of the escape pod's remains. She shone the flashlight at Redmayne but there was no sign of movement. "Good news," she said anyway. "The rescuers have arrived."

As she watched it land, *Lexington*'s rockets kicked up dust and small rocks that hid it from Georgia's view, but also showered her in fine particles. She didn't care. She was going to keep her promises to Jackson and Megan and live another day. Perhaps she was indestructible after all, although the pain from her bruised and battered body suggested otherwise.

She tried to stand but her joints had stiffened up and protested at the effort. Her right knee was heavily swollen and wouldn't bend at all. Using the twisted wreckage as a support she eventually managed to stand but the effort left her face covered in sweat. There was no way she would be able to walk unassisted. She could now see *Lexington* more clearly as the dust settled. The lights from the flight deck were shining like a towering lighthouse. She saw another light as the cargo bay door slid open, revealing the silhouettes of two astronauts and two speeders being lowered in the cradle. She told herself that one of the astronauts would have to be Mancuso but the other could be either Jackson or Megan. At that moment, Georgia hoped it was the Doctor, but she knew that Jackson would be desperate to ensure that she was okay.

With the radio transmitters smashed during the impact on landing, Georgia realized the only way to communicate her presence was with the flashlight. She waved it several times above her head and was rewarded by one of the astronauts in the cradle shining their light in return.

She waited patiently for the two astronauts to roll up. As they passed the wreckage of the escape pod, her personal comms channel sprang to life with the voice of Jackson. "Georgia, is that you? Are you OK?"

"Did we save the base?" were the first words she could think of.

"Yes, you're a hero again, sis. How do you expect me to be able to compete with you when you keep doing things like this?" As Georgia had suspected, Jackson was unable to find out if she was dead or alive. The relief in his voice was palpable.

Mancuso added, "we're waiting for formal confirmation that the Chinese ship was destroyed but we witnessed two of explosions. And Stockton says that his satellites are unable to locate *Taipei*. Where's Redmayne?"

"He's under this piece of twisted metal. I don't know if he's alive but I'm unable to get him out. Can you guys help? And where is Megan? I need painkillers."

Between them, Mancuso and Jackson made light work of lifting the twisted metal and rolling Redmayne onto his back. The small computer display on his wrist showed that the suit was still functioning, but no pulse was being registered.

"It looks as if he wasn't as lucky as you, Georgia," said Mancuso.

Georgia felt hollow. After all, Redmayne had saved her life and that of Alpha Base's crew. "I think this was what he wanted" she said. "There was no place for him at Alpha, or anywhere else. He told me he was ready to atone for what he'd done but I'm not convinced he was prepared to be kept locked up for the rest of his life."

"I hope you don't have any sympathy for him. He ended the lives of some good men because of his greed and selfishness," said Mancuso.

"Don't get me wrong, Joe. He deserved to be punished but I didn't want him to die for us. It's such a waste of a brilliant mind. Imagine what he could have achieved."

"I think we've done pretty well without him so far. I'll admit I'm grateful he helped to save the base but that's as far as I'll go. Do we take him back with us or bury him here?"

"I know you're eager, Joe but I think we should let Megan confirm that he's dead before we consider what to do with him!" Georgia replied. "Let's take him back to *Lexington* for the Doctor to take a look."

Jackson smiled. "Georgia, I don't know if anyone has told you, but you look like shit."

"Funny you should say that, little brother," she laughed. "Let's see how you look next time you carry out a daring mission. For that comment, you can lend me your speeder. You're walking back." And with that, she hobbled onto Jackson's speeder and made her way slowly toward *Lexington*.

Chapter 34

Less than two miles from the escape pod, a small craft hovered silently and invisibly. Its two occupants had been paying close attention to the events of the past few hours.

"You have shown incredible restraint, Grant. This was a supreme test of your abilities to not intervene with the events of your species, despite your friends being at risk of annihilation. You have done very well."

"Thank you, Falmas. You do me a great honor and your praise is important to me. However, I find it remarkable after your many years observing humans that you still fail to appreciate their capacity for ingenuity and survival. You're an intelligent species. Georgia Pyke's resilience in the face of adversity is without question. I had little doubt that she would succeed in overcoming the odds and therefore there was never any need for intervention."

Falmas looked perplexed. "Humans are like no other species we have encountered. You are complex, conflicted, territorial, you yearn for peace yet devote most of your time to violence and warfare. I don't believe another six thousand years will be sufficient time to understand your nature."

Grant stood up to stretch his legs. The nano-actuators in his hip and knee joints were slow to respond. A sure sign that they required further adjustment. "I'm sure that's what makes us such a fascinating species to study. Whereas I am quickly learning from you that intervention is not the right thing to do. Even though we have the power to assist, we are not gods. It is right that we should not intercede at the first sign of trouble. Of course," he added, "Georgia and I are exceptions to that rule. You made the right call in saving our lives."

Falmas acknowledged Grant's statement. "I remember not too long ago when you held fiercely different views to our having saved your life. You have come a long way since then. Yet I have been punished for my earlier discretions by being tasked with educating you in the ways of the Sentinels. I don't believe those responsible could have chosen a better way of reminding me that we are simply observers."

"Admit it," said Grant. "You secretly enjoy my company."

"I'm not sure 'enjoy' is the correct terminology. I have learned to tolerate your presence and your strange ways. Spending all my time with you is an... education!"

"I'll take that," replied Grant, who was still getting accustomed to his new body parts and not having human companionship. "You're not the easiest person to live with either. The important question for me is this. Do you think Georgia could be the one you've been seeking?"

Falmas was suddenly very defensive. "How do you know about that? The information is highly classified research and none of your concern."

Grant tried not to sound too smug. He didn't want to upset his new friend. "I told you we were resourceful. How can you not expect me not to discover the truth about this mission? It's been obvious for a while that there was more that you weren't telling me. Anyway, answer the question."

Falmas stared at him dumbfounded. "You are impossible." He finally nodded, slowly. "She could be, yes. I have requested the attendance of Jillnap to witness Georgia Pyke's behavior at first hand. He will be here within six months to commence his examination of her conduct. Only then will we know for sure."

Grant looked back at the view screen at an image of Georgia now being helped onto *Lexington*'s cradle. Involuntarily, he reached out a hand toward the screen longing to be able to speak with her again. But for now, the time wasn't right, and it wouldn't be in her best interests if he tried to warn her of what was to come. He'd met Jillnap twice. Neither occasion had been pleasant and, at the sound of his name, he felt a pang of fear for Georgia's safety. "Speedy recovery," he whispered to the final image of Georgia before the cargo hatch closed. "You're going to need all the energy you have."

<<<THE END>>>

IF YOU ENJOYED INCURSION

My Mars Frontier series charts the progress of human colonization on Mars. Book 1 of the series, Discovery, is available on Amazon now. Book 3 in the series will be published in January 2020.

DISCOVERY sees Mission specialist Georgia Pyke arrive on Mars with bold intentions to establish a legacy, unaware one of her colleagues has been holding a grudge for six years. How far is that person prepared to go to exact their revenge?

The mission quickly becomes a matter of life and death for the twelve astronauts as they struggle to establish a foothold on Mars. While Georgia and her crewmates fight the elements as well as their personal demons, something is lurking out of sight. Something that will change them forever.

? WHAT READERS ARE SAYING: ?

"This book is an easy read. It's well paced and sets the scene for the next books in the series. The characters are well formed, believable and very human. There is just enough technical talk to make it all seem real without turning the reader off. This is the first book I've read by this author and am looking forward to finding out what happens next! Highly recommended" – J. Bee

If you're looking for a fast-paced action adventure, get your copy of Discovery today!

Amazon US[1]
Amazon UK[2]

---

1.   https://www.amazon.com/dp/B07Z6NTP7F

2.   https://www.amazon.co.uk/dp/B07Z6NTP7F

GET EXCLUSIVE CONTENT

Building a relationship with my readers is the very best thing about writing. I occasionally send newsletters with details on my current projects, new releases and special offers.

And if you sign up to the mailing list, I'll send you a copy of Deception, my prequel to the Mars Frontier series. You can receive this novella, for free, by signing up at www.paulrixauthor.com[3]

---

3.   http://www.paulrixauthor.com

ABOUT THE AUTHOR

Paul Rix is the author of the Mars Frontier human colonization series. His online home is at www.paulrixauthor.com[4]. You can connect with Paul:

on Twitter at www.twitter.com/PaulRix8[5]

on Facebook at www.facebook.com/paulrixauthor[6]

or email at paul@paulrixauthor.com if the mood takes you.

---

4.   http://www.paulrixauthor.com

5.   http://www.twitter.com/PaulRix8

6.   http://www.facebook.com/paulrixauthor

Printed in Great Britain
by Amazon